T0366127

THE
DROWNING

THE DROWNING

E. J. STAUFFER

Copyright © 2017 E. J. Stauffer.

All rights reserved. No part of this book may be used or reproduced by any means, graphic, electronic, or mechanical, including photocopying, recording, taping or by any information storage retrieval system without the written permission of the author except in the case of brief quotations embodied in critical articles and reviews.

Archway Publishing books may be ordered through booksellers or by contacting:

Archway Publishing
1663 Liberty Drive
Bloomington, IN 47403
www.archwaypublishing.com
1 (888) 242-5904

Because of the dynamic nature of the Internet, any web addresses or links contained in this book may have changed since publication and may no longer be valid. The views expressed in this work are solely those of the author and do not necessarily reflect the views of the publisher, and the publisher hereby disclaims any responsibility for them.

Any people depicted in stock imagery provided by Thinkstock are models, and such images are being used for illustrative purposes only. Certain stock imagery © Thinkstock.

This is a work of fiction. All of the characters, names, incidents, organizations, and dialogue in this novel are either the products of the author's imagination or are used fictitiously.

ISBN: 978-1-4808-5217-4 (sc)
ISBN: 978-1-4808-5218-1 (e)

Library of Congress Control Number: 2017953469

Print information available on the last page.

Archway Publishing rev. date: 9/18/2017

CHAPTER 1

THE ALMOST FULL MOON REFLECTED OFF THE WATER AS IT cascaded onto the beach and ran several yards up the sand. The roaring rhythmic sound as the waves broke, the soft fragrant breeze carrying a slight scent of sweet smelling blossoms and the moonlight made the young honeymooning couple, Norman and Gwendoline, think of romance as they walked in their bare feet. Wearing shorts, they strolled along the shoreline in and out of the water. Neither wanted to think that in a few days they would have to return to real life and leave behind, paradise. Norm had his arm around her shoulder and his hand inside of Gwen's bikini top, massaging her breast. His other hand held their sandals. He was getting more and more excited as he thought of the two of them making love on the beach. Gwen's response when he voiced his thoughts was, "What if someone else is out walking along the beach and see us." She snuggled closer to him. When her hand brushed against the front of his shorts, she whispered into his ear with some urgency, "We are near our hotel, let's hurry back to our room."

Several minutes earlier and almost a hundred yards further along the beach in the direction they were walking, they did not see a man attack a young woman. He came up behind her and hit her hard on the back, knocking her down onto the sand. On her hands and knees, she spat out sand, struggled to catch her breath and to get up. The wind knocked out of her when she was hit, she was unable to call out. All that she could do was gasp as she struggled to pull oxygen into her lungs. He walked to her and kicked her hard in the side causing her to turn over onto her back as water running up the beach now engulfed her. She continued to gasp and tried to catch her breath as the receding water tried to wash her back into the ocean. For the first time, she was able to look at her attacker. There wasn't anything to see. He was tall, dressed in dark clothes and wore some sort of a full-face mask that covered his entire face except for his eyes. He reached down and grabbed her by the front of her blouse, the standard top that the female personnel at her hotel wore. She was a small woman compared to him. He easily could pull her toward him, close enough so that he could read her name tag in the moon light, Danni. He twisted a little to the side as he extended his left hand back to get a good swing at her. He punched her in the face. Reeling backward was too much of a strain on her blouse as the top button tore away and the remaining ones quickly followed. Before he could swing again, with his free hand he quickly grabbed the one side of her blouse with both hands. Danni began to fall away, as far as her torn garment would let her. He pulled hard on the cloth he held so that she began to spin and her blouse was pulled off one arm. He continued to pull causing her to continue to spin. Now he was able to pull the blouse completely away as her momentum caused her to fall onto the sandy beach.

He quickly walked to her, reached under her bra between her breasts, grabbed it and again pulled her toward him. She tried to call out when he slapped and punched her with a closed fist several times. In the moon light, blood running from her nose and mouth looked black as it blended with the black hair that fell across her face. He turned toward the ocean and dragged Danni into deeper water. He let go of her bra and both of his hands went around her throat as he squeezed. The water was deep enough so as the wave came in, he could not only strangle her but, also push her head under the water to drown her. But not yet. He removed his hands and lifted her head out of the water as the wave receded and washed the blood from her face. She ignored the irritation of the salt water on the cuts to her face and lips. Instead Danni gasped for breath and coughed, her calls for help were barely audible. "Please, please stop," she whispered. "Help," was lower than a whisper. He grabbed her hair and lifted her head, slapped her again causing the blood to flow. She fell forward and tried to crawl onto drier sand. He kicked her hard on the side again, rolling her over onto her back. His hands again went around her throat. After a short time, he removed them. Another wave broke and water went up the beach. He grabbed her under her bra again, lifted and begun to pull her into deeper water. Her bra broke and she fell into the water. Her small white breasts stood out against her well-tanned body but her nakedness was of little interest to him. He reached down, his hand went inside her skirt and he lifted her again. Her torn bra straps slipped off her arms as they hung down. Again, the masked man pulled her further into deeper water. She reached at him as best as she could and grabbed him by the wrist. Unable to break his hold of her skirt, she tried to scratch him. She tried to call for help but the damage he had done to her throat made it impossible for more than a whisper to come out of her mouth. In deep water now, he pushed her head under water, stifling even the whisper. After a moment, he pulled her out of the water. Danni gasped and coughed. He attempted to lift her again by her skirt, it ripped and she fell away into the water. Now down to her panties, she tried to get up. She was on her hands and knees as the water receded. The masked man walked closer to her from behind and put his hands around her neck, lifted her and squeezed. She tried to break free but was too spent to be able to do anything. Arms flailing, he lifted her to a standing position, as he pulled her head back. Hands firmly around the neck, he forced her down so that she sat on her behind. This time he was sure he was going to kill her. Only thing to decide, strangle her or drown her.

Coming along the beach Norm and Gwen were now close enough

to witness what was happening, but were mistaken in their first assessment. "She's almost naked. I can see her breasts. Looks like someone doesn't care if people are on the beach and see them," Norm said to Gwen.

Gwen wasn't so sure of what they were seeing. "I don't think they are in the throes of love making. It looks like he is strangling her!" she said to her husband and she yelled to the masked man, "Hey you, what are you doing!?" She removed Norm's hand and pulled him toward the two at the water's edge. Urging Norm, she said to her new husband, "Make him stop Norm!"

At the yell from someone on the beach, the masked man let go of the girl when he saw a man and a woman coming toward him. He turned and ran away. Danni collapsed and fell on her stomach as the water receded. Norm and Gwen went to Danni who they now saw lying face down in the wet sand. The two knelt beside the girl and again as a wave broke and water ran up the beach to engulf them, Norm lifted Danni's head out of the water "Is she dead?" asked Gwen.

Norm quickly turned her over and felt for a pulse. "She's alive, barely. Help me pull her further up the shore." They heard Danni cough and knew she was alive. "You stay here with her, I'll go to the hotel and get help," Norm said to Gwen, all thoughts of him and his new bride making love forgotten. Their attention now was on the life of this girl on the beach, keep her alive and get professional help.

The next morning standing outside Danni's hospital room was a good looking taller woman, about five foot ten, sex crimes detective, Christine Morse. She could be quite intimidating when she needed to be. Coming down the hallway a second pretty detective, Billy Winstin, approached her. Both were smartly dressed and could be any professional working women except that each had their police identification badges hooked on the pockets of their jackets. Both wore police directive loose fitting slacks with a light-colored blouse and were thankful that they weren't required to wear ties like the men. When Christine pulled her jacket back, her police pistol could be seen in a holster on her belt. "What do we know about this assault," Billy asked Christine. "I was called in this morning on the case. You will need to bring me up to speed."

"Right now, you know as much as I do, which is almost next to nothing," Detective Morse replied and then continued. "Two uniforms called it in last night and the lieutenant gave it to me. When I had gotten at the scene earlier, she had already been taken to the hospital. According to the EM's report, the girl was attacked on the beach in front of her hotel. They were not sure if he wanted to strangle her or drown her. CSI couldn't find anything on the beach. If there was anything there, incoming water would have washed it away or contaminated it."

"Was she raped," Billy wanted to know.

"No, according to the EM's that responded, they didn't think so," Christine answered. "We will know for sure once she is examined here at the hospital. Seems that she was only beaten. I asked for you because something similar happened to your sister and you take a special interest in these types of crimes."

"Thanks," Detective Winstin said. "I get a lot of satisfaction putting a guy like this away. Who found her?" she wanted to know.

"A honeymooning couple out for a late-night stroll saw what was happening, the woman shouted at the attacker, he bolted and ran down the beach," was the detective's answer.

"Any description?" Billy inquired.

"Not much. The two witnesses said the guy was in dark clothes and think he wore a mask. Couldn't see his face at all. It was night and they couldn't see much more. Not a big man, average build, maybe six feet tall was all that they could say," was Christine's reply.

"What about the girl?" again asked Detective Winstin.

"The guys who took the report said she couldn't say much, traumatized as well as beaten. The one name they were able to get out of her was Phillipe DeBain," Detective Morse answered. "The lieutenant would like for us to clear it quickly. Hotel doesn't want it to be known that people are unsafe and can be attacked on their beach. If it was this DeBain character and we can prove it and he is put away, everyone will be happy. A slam dunk case." After a moment, she said, "Shall we?" and she turned to the door and gently knocked on it as she pushed down on the handle. The door opened and in front of them stood a doctor. A nurse was tidying up around the girl on the bed.

"Detectives Christine Morse and Billy Winstin," Christine said to the doctor who met them at the door.

"We need to talk to her doctor. How is she?" Detective Winstin asked him in a quiet voice.

"She's pretty banged up, a bit of bruising, four cracked ribs and a slight concussion. The beating was serious but she is stable and should recover," the doctor said to them in hushed tones as he looked at his patient. The nurse finished and excused herself from the room. "She may be here for a week or longer. She will be hoarse for a while but hopefully that should also go away."

Detective Morse had to ask, "Hoarse?"

"The worst part was the strangulation. In my professional opinion, the guy was intent on killing her and would have if the couple on the beach had not interrupted him. A throat specialist will be working with her as soon as some of the bruising and swelling go down," the doctor told the two. "We hope any damage will not be permanent and she will have a complete recovery.

"Was she raped?" Detective Winstin asked the doctor.

"No," he replied.

"Doctor, can she talk? We need to ask her some questions about her attacker," Detective Morse said. "Get any information we can as soon as possible while it is still fresh on her mind."

"Yes, but don't expect long answers and don't tire her. Make sure not to excite her. Her larynx was severely damaged and shouldn't be stressed," the doctor said as he made a few notes on her chart and hung it at the foot of her bed, stepped to the side and would wait for the interview. He let it be known that he did not want his patient to be put under any undue stress and he would be there to make sure it wouldn't happen.

The two detectives approached the bed where Danniele (Danni) Kayleu was propped up against a pillow sucking on a piece of ice. She held a plastic glass in one hand that was full of ice chips, a bent plastic straw in it. Either it was hospital policy or someone had provided flowers that were in a vase on the bedside table. Besides the flowers was a pitcher of ice. Both detective Morse and Winstin saw what they believed was a young and pretty woman in her mid-twenties with long black hair. The parts of her that were visible were either bandaged or showed ugly purplish bruises. She had swollen, cracked lips. Her nose was bruised and had a bandage on it. Both eyes were discoloring. Her cheeks and fore head were bandaged. Her neck was wrapped in a bandage. The bandages could not hide the look of a youthful beauty who looked like any minute she would cry.

"Miss. Kayleu, we are police detectives, I am Christine Morse and this is Billy Winstin. We need to ask you some questions," Christine said as she bent over and was closer to the girl on the bed.

"Are you able to tell us about your attack?" Detective Morse asked her.

Struggling to get the words out, in a horse and raspy voice, not more than a whisper, they heard Danni say, "It was him, Phillipe."

"Phillipe who," Detective Winstin wanted to know as both detectives leaned closer to the patient on the hospital bed. Christine was allowing her partner to ask questions while she wrote in her note book what Danni said.

What the two detectives first believed was the patient about to cry, suddenly turned into a look of rage. She spit out in a strained rough and forced whisper, "Phillipe DeBain. He beat me," Danni paused and then continued in a calmer controlled voice, "before! He should be in jail!"

"How do you know that it was him? See his face, he say anything?" detective Winstin asked.

Danni was silent for a moment. Detective Morse broke the silence, "You say he beat you before. What's your relationship with him? How do you know him?" she asked in a low soothing voice.

"I went out with him once," she whispered as she took a sip of water from the glass and then a piece of ice from the glass. The cold piece of ice seemed help her throat, and again in the same hoarse strained voice she said, "He beat me up." She whispered around the piece of ice. "We went to court. He told the judge rough sex."

"Could it have been?" Detective Morse wanted to know as she began to ask questions about Miss Kayleu's previous accusations of DeBain beating her. "I read the original police report. He said rough sex and was acquitted by a judge."

"I told the judge we never had sex, period," Danni hoarsely whispered in reply.

"It couldn't be proved one way or the other. What happened?" the detective continued.

"Him and his slick lawyer were believed," Danni replied in a voice barely a little above a whisper. "They surprised me by asking questions that had nothing to do with my accusations and I blurted out some answers about my past that I shouldn't have. His lawyer convinced the judge that I had convinced myself and I believed that we never had sex."

"I read the report. You both passed a lie detector test," Detective Morse said to her. "Are you sure that it was him? You wouldn't be trying to get even with him, would you?"

"No, and I can't explain the test!" the hurt girl said after a moment as she struggled to get the words out. The two detectives saw the disbelief on the girl's face, that she would say something like that about a man to get revenge.

"Witnesses said it was dark and your assailant was dressed in dark clothes and they believed his face was covered," Detective Morse said as she tried to get a positive statement from Miss. Kayleu. "You couldn't have seen him." Her low voice said and her partner could hear the defeat, that the case would not be a slam dunk.

"It was him!" Danni tried to shout in a hoarse voice.

The doctor cleared his throat so that the two detectives look toward him. They saw him put both his hands out, palms down, moving them down, indicating that they should keep it down. They were exciting Danni.

"What were you doing on the beach alone late at night?" Detective Morse asked.

"Hotel got a call about one of our umbrellas being washed out to sea," Danni told the detectives. "Management sent me out to get it."

They would check on that, make sure Danni didn't plan to meet up with her assailant. "You didn't see him, did you?" Detective Winstin asked her in a low voice not really expecting an answer.

"I didn't have to see him to know it was him. Who else could it have been?" Danni said as her eyes became watery and tears began to form.

"I'd like to put him in jail, but we will need proof. Did you recognize his voice, his clothes? Something that could prove DeBain was your assailant?" the detective wanted to know.

All that the beaten girl could whisper was, "No! It was dark and I was fighting for my life! He never said anything."

Detective Morse calmly told her, "We will talk to him, but without anything more positive from you there's not much we will be able to do."

Struggling to whisper Danni said, "He was the same size as Phillipe."

At this point the doctor spoke, "I think you have gotten as much from her as you need. Time for her to rest and I believe you two should leave."

"If you think of anything, anything at all that can link your attacker to DeBain, let us know," Detective Winstin said to her. "I'll leave my card here on the table. We will keep in touch. In the meantime, concentrate on getting well." They thanked the doctor and left.

As they walked down the hallway Detective Morse uttered her thoughts. "It isn't going to be easy to prove DeBain was the assailant with no hard proof. Will most likely not even be unable to arrest him. All that they will be able to do was question him and see if he had an alibi."

CHAPTER 2

IT WAS SATURDAY MORNING TWO DAYS LATER AT THE HOTEL where Danni worked. Walking out to the pool area was Raymond Lakaa, a member of the hotel staff, a 'do whatever needed to be done' employee. He was a big man of dark complexion, typical of what one would think of someone who was a native from the south pacific. He wore the typical hotel blue shirt and tan shorts. Like Danni, he had a name tag that said his name was Raymond. Not that he was overweight, but that he was a big man, he filled his uniform and his shirt strained. It looked like that any moment his uniform's buttons would pop off.

He reached the pool area and began arranging chairs, tables and lounges around the pool. He opened several table umbrellas and set up several near the lounges, putting their aluminum poles in pre-cast concrete bases. He went to the storage hut where pool furniture and supplies were stored, returned with two armfuls of pillows and began scattering them amongst the lounges and chairs. Returning to the storage hut he placed two large piles of towels on the hut's counter. He soon returned to the pool attaching two aluminum pipes together that he had gotten, one with a pool skimming net attached to it. Walking to the pool he began to skim out debris that had been blown into it over-night. Coming from the hotel breakfast dining area was one of the hotel guests, Benjamin Knight, who he had developed a casual relationship with. Back home the guest worked for an unknown government agency that eliminated undesirables. He had a nickname, he was called The Magician because he could make people disappear. But now, he was in Hawaii on a vacation recovering from wounds he suffered in the Mid-east. He wore shorts and shoes, no socks, instead of sandals or tennis shoes and had on a flowery Hawaiian shirt. Raymond thought he looked quite the tourist. His hair was short and Raymond remembered how white he was when he arrived five days ago. Now this guest was showing a tan that would make friends back home be envious since it was still March. He wore sporty aviator dark glasses to finish off his appearance. When he neared the hotel staff worker, as usual, he struck up a short casual conversation and asked, "Tell me Raymond, why is it people want to sit around the pool when they have the whole Pacific Ocean a couple hundred yards from here?"

"Beats me sir, I think some of them just want to be seen or are getting a tan," Raymond answered him.

"Could do both of those on the beach," said the guest and he paused. In a moment, he continued talking to Raymond, "Thought you worked noon through the evening, you pulling double duty Raymond?" the hotel guest asked.

"Sort of Mr. Knight, hotel is shorthanded this week so I said I'd work more hours," he replied, "and tomorrow is Sunday, my day off."

"Don't be so formal, I told you that you can call me Ben." He hesitated for a moment before he continued, "You see Danni, tell her I really enjoyed the trip to the mountain top to watch the sunrise, and like she said, it was cold. The fishing charter she suggested was also fabulous, but no one caught anything the skipper said we should keep for the hotel chefs to prepare," he said to Raymond.

Raymond continued to skim the pool and said, "The boat captains rarely do. Hotel chefs have complained, don't want to spend the time needed to prepare a single fish." He stopped and turned to knock the skimming net into a trash can. He faced Knight and said, "Danni won't be around for a while."

"Why's that?" Knight asked.

"She's in the hospital," Raymond answered.

"What happened? She sick, have an accident?" Knight wanted to know.

"No sir Mr. Knight, I mean Ben. She was attacked and beaten up on our beach night before last. Police believe that the guy not only beat her but was intent on drowning her. Kept dragging her into the surf," said Raymond.

"Beaten!" said the astonished Knight. He couldn't believe what he had just heard. "How is she?" he wanted to know.

"I went to see her. She's pretty banged up but her doctor said she will be okay. Worst part, her attacker tried to strangle her. Injured her voice box. Most likely will have a hoarse voice for a while, maybe permanently, her doctor told Danni and me, when I visited her in the hospital," Raymond explained as he scooped a palm frond from the pool.

"Thought you said he tried to drown her," Knight said to Raymond.

"That too. Police were not sure which he intended to do. They assumed it was either or both, strangling and drowning," he said as he continued cleaning the top of the pool.

Knight asked, "Police get the guy?"

"No. According to her and witnesses, he wore some sort of mask, couldn't make an identification. Way he was dressed and the mask, police believe that the guy planned it. Not just a random attack," was Raymond's answer, "especially since a phone call to the front desk lured her out onto the beach at night. He was after her and wanted her."

"Sorry to hear about her. She was so nice to me, friendly and helpful. I liked her. Didn't know that someone disliked her enough to do something like that, want to kill her. Will she be back?" Knight wanted to know.

Raymond had finished skimming the pool so he stood, took apart the two-piece aluminum pole and unscrewed the net and removed it. He continued to talk to the hotel guest, "Not for a while. Physically she will be okay but I don't know ..."

Curious at Raymond's last answer, Knight had to ask, "Don't know what?"

"She thinks she knows who it was that attacked her, but no proof or evidence. Same guy that beat her a few weeks ago, and she believed was stalking her, Phillipe DeBain. Same guy accused of drowning his wife a while back but was not convicted," Raymond told Knight.

Knight thought about it for a moment before he said to Raymond, "She asked me to escort her home one night earlier in the week after the hotel beach luau. Was that why? She was afraid to be alone at night? Afraid of this guy?" he asked Raymond.

Leaning on his skimming poles Raymond answered him, "Probably. She must have trusted you. She was terrified of this guy DeBain, sure he had been stalking her, would hurt her again he got the chance. Wouldn't go anywhere at night unless someone was with her. Reported him to the police but they couldn't do anything without some sort of proof he was after her. He never called and never sent her a note of warning. Only thing, she did receive calls but the caller never spoke, just hung up. She believed it was him. Had to change her telephone number." Then with a little anger in his voice Raymond said, "I'd sure like to run into this guy some night in a dark alley. He wouldn't be beating anyone for a long time when I got through with him."

Knight asked, "You talking about this DeBain character or the guy who beat her?"

Raymond was quick to answer, "Far as I'm concerned, they are one and the same! If she believes it, then so do I."

Knight sized up the big man said, "I'd hate for it to be me. You must work out."

"A little," Raymond said, "and working on the docks for a couple of years didn't hurt." He stopped and then said as if he continued what he had just said, "Till I busted up my back. Got this job working at the hotel." He was still thinking along the same lines of how to protect the female employee and half uttered to himself when he asked, "I wonder how you would find a person that you could hire to kill someone? Wonder what it would cost?"

Knight heard him and thought the big man might be serious, so he answered him, "They are easy to find, work cheap, are easily caught and just as easily give you up. Keep out of it and if you are smart, you will let the police handle it."

CHAPTER 3

EARLY THURSDAY MORNING IN A HALLWAY THAT LED TO the morgue, two homicide detectives, Brian Amato and Moliki Malaki, were weaving and walking around the gurneys that had been parked in the hallway. Brian Amato was part Asian with thick black hair. His partner was a mixture of several ethnicities. He looked like he had a sly smile on his face and it could be said he was good looking. Both looked like they could handle themselves in a fight. When talking to a suspect, both could be quite intimidating. They talked as they headed toward the double doors. They were well dressed, wore light weight jackets and had on ties. Both were in their early thirties, about six feet tall and both looked like they were physically fit. Moliki was beginning to show a bit of stomach, especially when he buttoned his jacket. The buttons showed some strain on the jacket. When they reached the doors with the large red all capital letters, a warning sign, MORGUE AUTHORIZED PERSONEL ONLY, they stopped. "I hate coming down here," Detective Amato said as he put his hand on the door to push it open. He hesitated to open the door. "You hear guys say they could smell death at the scene. I'll tell you what death smells like …"

His partner had heard it before, so before he could finish what he began to say, Detective Malaki answered for him, "I've heard it a hundred times. I know, I know. It's a sharp smell that stings your nose.

Every time we come down here you say the same old thing. It's the chemicals you smell, especially alcohol. Don't want to smell it, put cotton up your nose. Probably won't sting your nose either."

"I know it's the chemicals, cotton will make me talk funny," Amato said to his partner. "Worse part is the smell, clings to my clothes just like cigarette smoke. I can smell it the rest of the day."

"It's in your mind. You imagine that you can smell it. Keep the cotton in your nose the rest of the day. Or think about what the flowers in your garden smell like instead of the morgue chemicals," said Malaki.

"It's not my imagination. Olana knows every time I come down here. The kids smell it too. The mutt won't come near me until I shower and change clothes. Explain that!" Detective Amato continued.

"I can't," Malaki said. "We are here. Are we going to just stand around and talk, or are we going in?"

Detective Amato was silent for a moment and then began to push one of the doors open, he stopped and said, "And it's chilly down here. What is so important about this body that the lieutenant wants us to look at it? Far as I am concerned it's just another case that needs to be solved. We could have just looked at some colored pictures of the victim and not have had to come down here. Could read the initial investigative report of the guys who found him and the coroner's report, and give our opinion of how and maybe why he died." Detective Amato had said more than once that he didn't mind looking at dead bodies, it was part of his job as a homicide detective. Even though, he didn't care for it. It was so final for the victims, there was no more future for them. Neither good nor bad. Just no more tomorrows. What he did mind, as he just told his partner, was looking at them in the morgue because of the smell. Real or imagined, he did not care for the smell. He thought it worse than at the scene, even a body that had had time to decay. When others would wear a mask, he would most of the time just ignore the smell. For some reason, he could not shake the morgue smell, real or imagined.

His partner didn't dislike coming down to the morgue except that Amato would always say something to him concerning the ME. Normally it would be after their visit. He would say something to the fact that she was single and not bad looking. Maybe could lose a little weight, but who doesn't? Had he ever thought about asking her out? She looked at him with those eyes that said she would like him to ask her out. Moliki always reminded Amato that he did not want his partner to help him with his love life. He would usually get out of the conversation by saying that he has not yet gotten over Wendy, even though it has been years since the divorce and they had parted on good terms. The divorce had been a mutual decision with no hard feelings on either part. Amato would follow up with he wanted to know if the fact that she worked in the morgue and handled dead bodies would bother him. When he always answered that it wouldn't, Brian Amato heard it as a yes, he should consider asking her out. He ignored what his partner had said to him and returned to Amato's complaint of the smell. "Maybe so partner. Don't let it bother you. We will check it out. Asked to come here to look at the body for a reason," Malaki answered. "Maybe there's a good reason for it. Maybe the lieutenant will want are opinion of how this guy was killed."

Detective Malaki added, "Or maybe give an opinion as to why he was killed."

"Not our worry. Detectives next in the rotation will get it and they can answer any and all questions concerning it," Detective Amato replied.

Detective Amato knew that he would have to enter the morgue so he went through the door he had pushed open. The two detectives entered the morgue, saw the coroner/medical examiner, Nikki Collings, at her desk, and walked to her. She was in her mid-thirties, could afford to lose a few pounds, as Detective Amato had indicated in the past, but she was not terribly overweight or what one would consider, fat. If she were a guy, she would be thought of as stocky. She had short, striking

blond hair that came out of a bottle. She was pretty, but turned most
men off when they learned what she did for a living. She liked her job
and took it serious and would chastise any detective who would make
a crack about the dead they had been viewing or were about to look at.
"What do you have for us Doc?" detective Amato asked her in a friendly
voice. He sniffled and then sneezed. Both were for his partner's benefit.

She rose, didn't say a word, just motioned to the two that they
should follow her and she walked toward where bodies were stored.
"Over here," she answered the detective as she walked to the drawers.
The two had accompanied her; and when she stopped, they stopped.
Nikki grabbed hold of a drawer handle without looking at the drawer's
label and slid the drawer out with ease. It contained a body with a white
sheet over it. She pulled the sheet off to reveal a very badly bruised and
disfigured body of a man, from his head down to his toes.

"Christ! What a mess. What do we have Nikki? Looks like a hit and
run?" Detective Malaki said to her.

Detective Amato bent down and looked at the right hand of the
dead man. He straightened, took a pair of rubber gloves out of his coat
pocket and put them on. That done he lifted the right hand and felt it
and the wrist, turned it over and repeated the same process on the back
side of the hand. He continued to feel the man's arm up to the shoulder.
His partner and the corner didn't say anything as they watched him.
He stopped examining the hand and arm, he walked around the man
on the drawer slab to the other side, lifted and began studying the left
hand the same way. He looked at the chest, poked it with his finger being careful to stay away from where it had been cut open by Nikki. He
straightened up, removed the rubber gloves, turned to Nikki Collings
and confidently said, "He was a jumper. Most likely not higher than
four or five stories, why his wrists are broken. Don't understand why
neither arm is broken. Broke both hands when he put them out to break
his fall, then his chest hit and broke a few ribs. Arms should also have
been broken if higher. The chest is quite bruised and I can see where

at least a rib bone broke through the skin when he hit the ground. The rest of his body was bruised or broken in the fall. Most likely fell in an uneven area, possibly a rocky area, why he is so bruised other parts of his body. Could have been thrown out of a plane and hit the sand, but I doubt it. He would be more smashed if from higher. Question is, did he jump, accidently fall, or was he pushed?"

Nikki stood close to Moliki when she answered, "Harbor boys pulled him out. A dock worker saw him floating against a dock pier and called the police. Condition of the body they thought a floater that had been hit by a boat and cut by the prop. First glance, I thought so too until I began to examine him. All of you are wrong," the coroner said to the detectives.

"If we are all wrong on how he died, what was it?" asked Detective Amato as he looked closer at the body.

"He was systematically beaten, most likely with a club of some sort. Could have been a hammer. In my opinion, most likely a baseball bat. See the almost perfect round bruises and round breaks where the flesh had been broken. The end of a bat would do that," she told the two detectives as she pointed to several bruises.

"What do you mean when you say systematically beaten Doc?" asked Detective Malaki.

"Where do you want me to start, head and go down or feet and go up?" she asked.

"An overview Nikki," he told her.

"Found traces of duct tape on his wrists and wood slivers in his palms, both pushed into his skin. He was taped up when it happened, and if I had to guess, I'd say he was taped to the arms of a wooden chair. Broken toes, feet, fingers and hands. Both knee caps broken. Ruptured spleen and kidneys. Ribs broken on both sides of his chest, one bone pushed into a lung, a broken skull and concussion. His jaw was broken and teeth knocked out. Numerous bruises other parts of his body. One ear was cut off, maybe as a souvenir. You catch the guy who did this, he may still have it, kept it as a souvenir," she told the two detectives. "Want me to go on?" she asked.

"No, we get the picture," Amato said. "You sure fish or some other ocean creature didn't bite or chew off his ear?"

"No. Too clean. It was cut," the coroner answered the detective.

"So, what killed him?" Brian wanted to know.

"In my professional opinion, it was a combination of all of the above. He was pounded, beaten, until he died. Hit in all the right places that would hurt but not kill him until the final blow, a hard one near the back of his head," the coroner said as she began to recover the body. "X-rayed it to show the fractured skull and the smashed neck vertebrae if it needs to be shown in court. Want to see it?"

"No. Sounds like a psycho nut case did it, someone with a strong stomach," Detective Malaki said. "Maybe it was done to send a message to others, drug peddlers or loan shark clients. Any other people that would need a message sent."

Detective Amato waited a moment before he added, "Or someone who really hated him, wanted to make him suffer."

Nikki Collings continued to talk, "Condition of the bruises and the body, it happened the day before yesterday, Tuesday, possibly late Monday. Being in the water, it has washed away all the blood and lessened the bruising color. The various discolorations of the bruises, I'd say it took place over an hour, give or take. Somebody wanted him to suffer for a while, but not too long. I've had him on the table now for two days. Most likely dumped in the water shortly after he died. As you called them, ocean creatures didn't have time to work on soft flesh parts. No attempt to hide him. Whoever did this didn't care if he was found. Probably driven to the docks and just dumped in the water same day that he was killed. Most likely at night, wait until dark so that the perpetrator wouldn't be seen. If he was, difficult to identify."

"Or thrown overboard from a boat," Malaki said not limiting how the victim got in the water at the docks.

She smiled at him and said, "That's a possibility. No one would hear him scream if on a boat, but where would the wooden chair come from?"

"A large ship, the captain could have one in his quarters," Detective Amato said. After a short silence, he asked, "If we were to find the boat and captain's chair, could the wood splinters found in his hands be tied to it?"

"Not my area of expertise, but I'd say a good chance. His blood and flesh would have been forced into the wood, easy to identify. I've picked them all out and will save them," she answered the detective.

"Do you have an identity Nikki?" Detective Amato continued.

"Can't tell from his face but I believe that he was a handsome man at one time. Had to wait a day for his fingers to dry out before we could roll his prints, and then were able roll three whole ones and a lot of partials because of the condition of his hands. Ran them and found out he is in the system, Phillipe DeBain," she told the two detectives.

"Well, well, well! Gonna' be some people pleased to hear about this," Detective Malaki commented.

"Lot of people hated him, lot of possible suspects," Detective Amato said as he thought about what he had heard, and read about DeBain. "Lot of people to interview, possible leads must be followed up on. Kominski and Trout will have a lot of suspects." They were next on the homicide rotation schedule and he knew it would be their case.

"Maybe it will be an open and shut case, easy to solve," his partner said in response.

"Kominski and Trout should be so lucky, but I don't think so." Detective Amato said to the coroner, "Could save them a lot of time if you were to list the death as a fall or a hit and run."

"Never happen,' She said as she began to put the sheet over the body. "I wouldn't do anything like that and the lieutenant knows. Soon as his identity was established, got word from him to rush the autopsy. Put it ahead of others that were scheduled. He said to send you to see him in his office after you talked to me. Lieutenant wanted you to see the body, know why the police are looking for his murderer and what his assailant had done to the victim. My best guess is that somehow the two of you are going to be involved."

Nikki was pushing the drawer back into its space as the two detectives headed toward the door. They both were silent but Moliki could see a smile on his partner's face. When they were through the double doors Moliki had to ask, "What's so funny? What are you smiling about?"

"Don't ask. Nothing that would interest you, you don't want to know," was his partner's reply.

After several steps Moliki said, "Tell me anyway."

There was some hesitation on Amato's part before he said, "When I saw you standing beside Nikki I thought that the two of you made a good-looking couple."

"You're right. I shouldn't have asked."

The two detectives walked through the squad room to Lieutenant Karawa's office. They could see him sitting at his desk. Detective Amato knocked and opened the door. Lieutenant Karawa, a small intense, no nonsense looking man looked up from behind his desk, saw the two and waved them in. Detective Amato said, "You wanted to see us lieutenant."

"Take a chair," the lieutenant said. "Nikki bring you up to speed on DeBain?"

"Yes," replied Detective Malaki.

"What is your initial response," the lieutenant asked.

Detective Malaki was the first to answer as he pushed back in his chair and in a relaxed easy manner said, "Seems like his past has finally caught up with him. He was tortured and then killed."

"Beaten to death, am I correct?" the lieutenant asked.

"Yes, from what Nikki said and showed us. Kominski and Trout will have work to do, but sounds like it will be easy to solve. One of the people who didn't like him will eventually be a suspect and confess."

"Detectives Kominski and Trout have been taken off the case, you two are taking over." Both detectives showed surprise at the lieutenant's statement. They knew that there was a good reason why the investigation was taken away from the two detectives who caught the case, given to them and that the answer would soon be coming from the lieutenant.

Amato accepted what the lieutenant said as if he knew and replied, "We will give it a quick look though, follow up on our leads, do our best," knowing that the lieutenant would expect nothing less.

"I want more than your best. I want a complete and thorough investigation and a daily update on your progress," Lieutenant Karawa told his two detectives.

"A lot of people think that he was a piece of crap. Why the urgency, lieutenant?" asked Detective Malaki. He had sat upright in his chair and knew that what the lieutenant had just told them meant that he was serious. This was not going to be a simple murder case but maybe had other implications.

Lieutenant Karawa said, "DeBain was a business partner with Cole Bennett in the West South East Trading Company."

Detective Amato had gotten the same unspoken message from the lieutenant that Malaki had, he said, "Catchy name, but who is Cole Bennett and his company? Never heard of either." Both waited but didn't have long to wait for an explanation.

Lieutenant Karawa addressed both of his detectives and said, "Cole is the half-brother of the governor. Took his mother's last name, Bennett. The company was to ship from the Far East to the mainland or here to the islands. I don't know how the governor found out about DeBain, hasn't been reported in the papers, but he has already called the chief and the chief wanted to know who would be handling the investigation. I told him I was putting two of my best on it. When I had said that, both of your names were mentioned by the chief. Need I say more?" The lieutenant as well as everyone else in the squad knew that the two detectives had more cases closed as anyone else. When neither said anything, they waited and the lieutenant continued. "The chief wants to keep the governor up to date on anything you two may uncover. I don't need to tell you that you should keep the governor's name out of it if possible. Only if there is some concrete evidence that would implicate him do I want him mentioned. Am I clear?"

Both detectives nodded their heads yes when Malaki asked, "Why do you think the governor is so interested in a half-brother's murdered business partner?"

"My guess," said the lieutenant, "is the money in the company. A lot, several hundred thousand, according to the chief, and the governor doesn't want a half-brother involved in a murder case. Talking to the chief, don't know how he or the governor knew, both believe he was killed for the money or gave up the money to stop the beating. They said it's missing. Start with the governor's half-brother, Cole. He's a bartender at the Beach Parrot's Roost. Question him and see what you can get."

CHAPTER 4

THE DETECTIVES DROVE TO THE BEACH PARROT'S ROOST bar. It was away from the island's major hotels and it wasn't near the water. Local regulars and a lot of navy personnel were its frequent customers. The owner knew a lot of them and would call them by their first name. It was not a tacky bar nor was it high end, it was somewhere in between. It was quite a theme bar though. The interior walls and an area around the bar were decorated with a pirate theme, pictures of galleons, cutlasses, skull and cross bones flags, tackle blocks with ropes, torn sails, and a ship's wheel among other things. Behind the bar, at its center on a shelf, was a large cage, and in it sitting on a perch, was a parrot, a scarlet macaw. When the two detectives entered the establishment, they saw about a half dozen customers sitting at the bar. They were not surprised that people this early in the day were drinking. Some people needed coffee in the morning to get going, and some needed a drink. They walked toward the bar and were approached by an elderly black bar tender who believed the two detectives were customers. As they neared the bar they heard the parrot squawk. "Looks like the one loose in my neighborhood, a scarlet macaw," Detective Amato said and he flashed his badge. "We are detectives, here to talk to Cole Bennett. I am Detective Brian Amato and this is Moliki Malaki."

The bar tender turned and called to the end of the bar, "Cole, police want to talk to you. I'll cover for you. Why don't you go to a booth in the rear?"

Cole was a thin man in his mid to late fifties, not very tanned, and most likely spent a lot of time indoors. He walked around the end of the bar and waited for the two police men to reach him and the three of them went to a rear booth and sat. After introductions, Detective Amato said to him, "Have some questions about you and your partner, Phillipe DeBain."

"I'll help in any way that I can, I heard what happened to him," Cole said to the two detectives.

Malaki said, "Tell us about him and your business."

Cole started right in, "Not much to tell, we were just getting started. We had been talking and planning for over a month. Got a DBA for our company and its name registered. Phillipe was making all the arrangements to lease cargo containers and shipping. What we were going to ship came next. He was talking to and making arrangements with several Chinese, South Korean and Malaysian middlemen."

When he finished, Detective Amato said, "Sounds like he was doing all of the work. What were you doing?"

"That's easy," said Cole, "he was the doer, I was the money." He continued in an excited and desperate voice, "I checked, it's all gone! I checked in our office safe and at the bank, nothing! We shouldn't have spent anything yet. He was just talking and setting things up. No contracts or promises had yet been made."

Malaki asked, "What kind of money are we talking about?"

Cole didn't hesitate to answer, "Two hundred and forty thousand. I want you to find it, I want it back! It was all the money I had in the world. An inheritance from my step grandfather, father of my mother's husband."

Detective Amato asked, "You think he was killed for it? Robbed?"

"Yes!" Cole said. "He was beaten wasn't he, forced for the combination of our safe, tortured for it, beaten until he gave it up and then killed!"

Detective Malaki wondered how everyone seemed to know about DeBain being beaten to death and it hadn't been reported in the paper or on the news. Had to come from the ME's office. He intended to say something to Nikki about it. He answered Cole, "That's a definite possibility, but we need to check into everything. Police, you reported the money stolen to, said no evidence he was killed in your office. Had to be somewhere else. Who would have known about the money?"

"No one," Cole replied to the question.

"You keep it in the safe," asked Detective Amato.

"No, the Honolulu State Bank. Either one of us could take it out," responded Cole.

Detective Malaki wrote down the name of the bank and asked, "So, if you didn't take the money, it had to be Phillipe." He waited a moment before he asked, "You didn't take it, did you? Try to get out of your partnership?" Detective Malaki was the one who usually accused people and let them deny the accusation.

Cole showed surprised by the question when he answered, "Of course not!"

"Anyone you can think of that he may have told?" continued Detective Amato. "Someone who didn't like him, he wasn't beaten for the money but maybe he gave up the money to get them to stop?"

Detective Malaki asked, "Could he been involved in the drug trade? Beaten over a deal that went sour?"

"Not that I would have known about. Phillipe stayed away from drugs. Thought they were trouble and a sure way to jail. Wasn't he beaten for the money?" asked Cole.

"We don't know for sure," said Detective Amato. "Did he gamble?

Cole answered him, "Like drugs, not that I knew of. I hired a reputable private investigator over a month ago to check him out. There was no evidence that he did either, drugs or gamble. Had to be for the money, right!?"

"We don't know. What is the name of the private investigator?" Amato continued. "We will need to talk to him."

"James Minot," Cole answered. "I found his name was in the book. Used to be with the FBI. When he retired, moved here, started his own private investigation business."

"We have to check all possibilities," said Malaki as he wrote down the detective's name. "He did have quite a checkered past, made a few enemies. One of his past acquaintances was just getting even, and well, he gave up the money to get them to stop."

"All of the things he was accused of, none were ever proven. Never jailed. Seemed like bad luck followed him around," said Cole. "The private investigator checked him out. I think he did a thorough job."

"Mr. Bennett, forget about the money for the moment. Anyone ever threaten him, hate him enough to kill him? Maybe someone he was afraid of?" Detective Amato asked.

"Only two come to mind. Talk to Bobby Hee, a local musician," Cole said. "Heard he threatened to kill Phillipe he ever went near his sister again. Said DeBain got in a fight with his sister and she hit him first. He belted her around a little. Hee said his sister never would have fought with DeBain. Believed he liked to hit her. Got into a tussle with him and blows were thrown. Police were called. Neither would press charges so both were warned. Then there was Doctor Pepper. Rumor I heard was that he hired some guy from Philly to kill Phillipe. Don't think either would have done it, had to be for the money and they wouldn't have known about it. If either of them did it, if for revenge or as a warning, it makes sense that he would give up the money to have them stop. But they didn't." Malaki wrote down both names Cole gave him in his note book.

"If what you say is true, and he was beaten for the money, he would have had to have it on hand, and not in the bank," Detective Amato said. "Did you keep in an office safe?"

"No, like I said, in the bank. Checked with the bank and found that he withdrew it. He must have put it in our safe in the office we share," Cole Bennet replied.

"No way would the bank give it to him if he looked beaten. Would have aroused too much suspicion, and the way the body was broken, wouldn't have been able to walk," Detective Amato continued.

Malaki asked, "When was the last time you saw DeBain, talk to him?"

"Saw him on Sunday. He was excited but showed no signs of a beating. I asked him about the bruise he had on his cheek. Said he ran into a shelf in our office. I opened the bar at seven on Monday. He called me early to tell me about the contract we were having drawn up by our lawyer. Told me he would be seeing our lawyer later that day and Phillipe told me that he would run it by me Wednesday in our office. We set a time to meet, ten o'clock," Cole told him. "Told him I couldn't wait, wanted to see him on Tuesday. He said no, and I couldn't reach him. He had to go to the big island and I'd have to wait. Wouldn't return until Wednesday. On Wednesday, he never showed up for our meeting. I came back to work and called him about every ten minutes. First, I called our office, got no answer. Same for his apartment and cell phone. Late Wednesday, I became concerned and worried. That is when I checked our account and safe. Found the money gone. My first thought was that he took our money and ran away with it. Called the police and reported it stolen. They said that they would investigate and search for him. The next day the police called me and said he was dead! It looked like foul play. They had no idea about the missing money."

"That is what we are investigating, the foul play, he was murdered. Maybe we find the murderer, we might find the money. Now tell us," and he pushed his pad across the table to Cole Bennett, "write down the addresses, DeBain's, your office, your lawyer's and the private detective who Cole had hired.

While Cole wrote, he said, Jason Witcomb, of 'Witcomb and Johnson Law', and the investigator Minot. "Don't know Minot's address. Both are here on the island," Cole told him and handed back his note pad. "He knew Witcomb from the past when he represented

Phillipe in some sort of law suit over his dead wife's will. Phillipe lived
in a new development, Sunny Palms. Don't know the number."

"That's okay. We will find it. Any other people that DeBain was
friends with that might be able to shed a little light on him and his
movements, maybe give us more of his background," Detective Amato
added.

"We were planning and meeting regularly but we never talked
much about our past or our friends. Never met any, don't know if he
had any," was Cole's answer. "He never mentioned any friends or people
that he knew," Cole continued. "Only ones I knew of were the ones he
had gotten in trouble with or the ones the private detective came up
with. He would have a list of people that DeBain knew."

"He ever mention any girl friends?" Detective Amato asked as soon
as Cole finished.

"No," replied Cole.

"How about boyfriends? Was he gay?"

Again, Cole replied in the negative. "If DeBain was seeing anyone,
male or female I didn't know about it. Neither of us talked much about
our private lives."

"He a private person? Sounds like it," Amato said.

"Don't know, we were not friends, didn't hang out. All we did together was have lunch and we discussed our business venture. I thought
of us as a professional partnership. Tried to keep it that way," Cole again
answered. "I know he lived on Maui for a while. That was in the private
investigator's report and he liked to hang out at that after-hours place,
'Leo's'. Ate at least a half dozen different restaurants for lunch."

Detective Malaki pushed his note pad to Cole and told him to write
down the restaurant names and anywhere else that he might think of
where Phillipe may have gone, anyone he knew, names he may have
mentioned. They continued to talk to Cole hoping that someone might
come to mind as he began to write down places and the two people who
he already mentioned.

"Know what he did in his spare time? Any hobbies, clubs he belonged to? Everything and anything about his life could be a lead we should follow up on," Detective Malaki said.

"The private investigator I hired to check him out was only concerned with his past legal problems. Except for the two people I mentioned, that's it, far as I know about him and his life," Cole Bennett replied.

"How did you two meet? Someone introduce you who we should talk to?" Detective Malaki asked.

"I'd have to say we met by chance about three months ago. You know that doughnut and coffee shop everyone talks about that advertises that supposedly it has the best coffee on the island?" When DeBain heard a half-hearted yes from Amato he continued. "The first and only time I ever stopped in there, that morning I met him. I was having a cup of coffee when I asked the guy across the counter from me if there was any cream in the pitcher near him. The guy was Phillipe DeBain. He passed the pitcher to me and we began talking. He had all these grand ideas about becoming a trader, buy goods in the East and shipping and selling them in the U. S. He told me of all his plans, only thing he needed to get started was the money. He was looking for investors."

They spent an additional half hour talking about DeBain and got more background on both him and Cole Bennett. "You think of anything, give us a call. Here's my card," Detective Amato said as he handed over his card.

The two detectives got up to leave when Malaki asked, "Why the pirate and parrot theme? Wouldn't something more islandy, or maybe Asian be more appropriate for the bar?"

Cole told him, "He's the owner," as he pointed at the guy behind the bar, "moved here from Jamaica so wanted that sort of a feel. Likes to take the parrot out and let it sit on his shoulder. Some patrons expect it."

"You didn't accidently happen to mention to him," and Detective Amato pointed to the man tending bar, "what you were planning?"

"He knew what we were planning but not that we had the money. Only thing I said to him was that my partner had been killed. Not once did I mention the money, not even after I learned Phillipe had been killed," Cole Bennett replied.

"We will talk to him anyway," Detective Malaki said and the two detectives went to the bar and motioned the bar tender over. Their talk to him proved unproductive. They found out that DeBain never came to the bar. The bar owner didn't recognize DeBain's photo.

When they were leaving the bar, Detective Amato said to his partner, "Let's check with his lawyer, see what he can tell us what may have happened on Monday, then on to the latest incident, Booby Hee. Will be easy to find. Only one talent agency on the island. If he was any good it would represent him. I don't know where they are located but they maybe can get us in touch with him, an address."

The detectives found the Witcomb and Johnson Law office located in an upscale high-rise and was on the top floor. They took the elevator to the law office floor and went into the firm's reception area where they were greeted by a male receptionist. They showed identification and asked to see Jason Witcomb. The receptionist touched a button on his telephone and in a moment, they could hear him say that there were two detectives here and wanted to talk to him. There was a pause in the receptionists talk and then the detectives were told that he was currently in conference with a client and it may be five minutes or longer before he would be able to see them. They should have a seat. Detective Malaki became absorbed with an article he had begun to read, of about all things, white tail deer hunting in West Virginia in a *Field and Stream* magazine. No deer in Hawaii his partner reminded him and commented on the office. "The firm must be doing well to be able to afford an office like this." Before Moliki could finish the article the receptionist told them Mister Witcomb would see them now and he pointed to a hallway and told them the conference room door would be open. They were invited in by a young woman, Jane Stein, who wore black framed glasses with her brown hair pulled back tight. Loose blouse and slacks prevented anyone from seeing if she was shapely or not. She gave the impression that she was all business and they would soon learn she was an intern. She would attend their meeting. Mister Witcomb was standing beside the conference table, early forties, smartly dressed in a suit, and wearing highly polished shoes. What looked out of place was his tie, it looked like it was covered with a series of panda bears. As soon as introductions were made he and the intern sat and asked them to join them and could he get them something to drink. When they declined, he informed them that his intern, Miss. Stein, would be taking notes during their meeting. Before they began talking he gestured with a thumb to his tie and explained that his seven-year-old daughter bought it for him. The detectives believed that he most likely wore ties that were picked out by his daughter and felt he needed to explain them since they stood out against his more formal conservative dress. Then he wanted to know how he could help them.

Detective Amato quickly said that they were here to get background information on one of his clients, Phillipe DeBain. Mister Witcomb said, "You know I cannot divulge anything the two of us may have discussed. Is this about the woman accusing him of beating her on her hotel's beach?"

"Not here to find out anything about what the two of you discussed that would be private. Your client has been murdered and we are investigating it," Detective Malaki said. If Mr. Witcomb was shocked about DeBain's death, he did not show it. "We were told by his partner that he was to see you Monday morning, the day it is believed he may have been killed. Want to know if you saw him, why he wanted to see you and where he may have gone afterward or anyone he planned on meeting later that day."

"Yes, I saw him just after eight, first thing in the morning. He was here for two reasons. First, the firm had drawn up a simple contract for buying, shipping, storage and selling of goods bought in China, South Korea and Malaysia. If it met with his approval our firm would be on record as his legal representative and advise him. The firm had already registered their new business and drew up a contract between him and a Mr. Bennett, his partner. They were to be partners and the contract spelled out the responsibilities of each." Jason Witcomb picked up the telephone on the conference table and quietly spoke into it and then continued. "The second reason he was here, he said he had been questioned by the police because he was accused by the woman I just mentioned, of beating her, and if need be, would I represent him. I'd done it in the past. Miss. Stein here can verify the meeting."

The detectives looked at her when she said, "For some reason he thought that this woman had it in for him. Already had him arrested for beating her not too long ago. He was found innocent and felt she was fixated on him."

Mr. Witcomb added, "DeBain wanted to meet with Miss. Stein later over drinks. Told him we do not meet with clients outside the office and I told him that I would represent him. I advised Miss. Stein she should stay away from him and not to talk to him outside the office, not even talk to him on the telephone except that she would gladly set up an appointment to come to our office."

Miss. Stein said that she was in total agreement with office protocol and informed DeBain she would be happy to talk to him but only in the office with Mr. Witcomb present.

"Did he say where he was going after you talked or what he might be doing?" Detective Moliki asked.

"Yes. He said something about going to the big island. He was going to look at some land to buy on Hawaii," Mr. Witcomb replied.

Detective Moliki followed up with, "He mention who he was going to talk to about the land or where it was located?".

"No, and I didn't ask for more information and he didn't offer any. If he did want us to represent him as his lawyer when and if he bought some land, he would get back in touch with me," was the lawyer response. "I thought our meeting was over and got up and went to the door."

Miss. Stein said, "That was when he mentioned to me that he saw it advertised, didn't say where, but it was in the interior of Hawaii. If he bought it, he might have a house built. I'd always be welcome to come and visit him. When I shook my head no, he got up and joined Mr. Witcomb."

"I never saw or heard from him again and I do not believe that Miss. Stein did either," Mr. Witcomb said. There was a knock on the door and it was opened. A woman entered and handed Mr. Witcomb a file folder. He took it as the woman left and handed it to Detective Amato. "Here is a copy of their partnership agreement and the contract for their company. Don't believe that you will find anything incriminating in either."

While his partner leafed through the documents handed to him, Detective Malaki asked, "He say who he was going meet, who he was meeting when he left here?"

"No idea," Mister Witcomb replied.

"Did he ever mention anyone else, other than his partner Mr. Bennett?" Detective Malaki asked.

"Not that I can remember," was Mr. Witcomb's reply.

"He say anything else to you Miss Stein?"

"No. It may mean nothing, but he had a bruise on his left cheek, more on his left jaw. He didn't say anything about it and I didn't ask," she answered the detective.

Mr. Witcomb continued, "Gave him a copy of the contract and told him to look it over with his partner. He folded it and put it in his pocket. I walked him to the outer reception office, not another word, that was about eight fifteen. We shook hands and he left. On the way through the reception area I did see him on his cell, no idea who he was talking to or what they may have talked about."

When they left the law firm's office building they decided to show his picture around the building and at businesses and shops along both sides of the street. None of the people they talked to had remembered seeing him either coming into their establishments or just walking by. That early in the morning many shops and businesses weren't yet open.

When they got back to their car Detective Malaki asked his partner, "Could the cheek bruise be a warning of what to expect if DeBain didn't ..." and he never finished what he had begun to say.

"Didn't what?" Brian Amato asked.

"Don't know," Moliki said. "Just thinking out loud. We can't forget what Cole said about him being beaten for the money. Maybe the lieutenant is right, it will come back to the money. It always does." He was silent for a moment before he said, "I agree with you, let's go to the private investigator's next."

A call to the station on their way to the private investigator got them the address of the recording company that represented Bobby Hee. They decided to stop there first. They came away with nothing relevant.

When they arrived at the private detective's address they found that his office was in his house. Not a big house on a small lot, but a view of the ocean at least a mile away. When they showed their credentials, he invited them into his house, then into a small room that served as his office. The walls were decorated with framed commendations and they could see a law school degree. Mr. Minot was a big man, crew cut gray hair, dressed in typical Hawaiian clothes, sandals, shorts and a flowery shirt. He asked them to sit. The two detectives declined a drink offer. "My wife insisted we buy it because of the view," he told them and said he didn't argue with her because there wasn't much of a yard that he would have to be responsible for. He asked what he could do for the two of them.

Detective Amato said, "We are investigating the murder of Phillipe DeBain. His partner, Cole Bennett, said he hired you to do a background check on him. What can you tell us?"

The private investigator put on glasses and opened a file folder on his desk and said, "Mr. Bennett called me this morning and told me he had been killed. There were no details. He also said I should help you in any way I could if you should drop by. Here is my thorough work up on DeBain, going all the way back to his college days where he got a degree in business. I was unable to find much of anything before that and didn't think that if I could, it would be relevant to Mr. Bennett's request. I gave all this information to Mr. Bennett. Here is a copy of my investigation, all of the people I talked to, it will save you some time."

"Anyone or anything that stood out that we should look at?" Detective Malaki asked. "Nothing in particular but everything in general," the investigator said. "He had a number of run-ins with the law and several arrests for abuse. Usually it was over the trouble he had with someone, a woman. Never convicted of any that were major enough to warrant jail time that I could find. All the arrests were of a personal nature and his trouble with women starting when he was in college up until he was accused by the grand parents of the missing Oh girl. His former college roommate said he was accused of date rape. It, like all the other problems with the law up to the Oh family accusing him of murder, were never proven. The girl in college refused to prosecute and the case was dropped. The roommate asked to be relocated and was. He never saw or had heard of DeBain again. The Oh girl was never found and the case is still open. Then there was the secretary at his first job. Had him arrested, said he forced himself upon her and slapped her around a little and assaulted her. Then she tells the police she is pregnant and blames him. Afraid and too embarrassed to come forward earlier. Again, not convicted when the baby's DNA said it wasn't his. It's all here in his file."

"What's not in the file that you can tell us?" Detective Amato asked him. "Did he gamble, do drugs?"

"Neither as far as I could find out," the private investigator answered.

"Any other vices?" detective Maliki asked.

"Not that I could find," investigator Minot said, then added, "I'll sum it up for you the same way I did for Mr. Bennett. The business degree said he was qualified to manage the trading company they were thinking of starting. I did not come across anything in his past that said he was dishonest or would steal, but I wouldn't trust him not to steal from the business they were planning if he got the chance. Only incident I could find concerned money he had been paid for a job he failed to complete and was sued for. After a while he returned the money paid him and even that judgment was satisfied. I told Mr. Bennett, when and if they got the money to start up, he would be wise if he kept a close eye on the money and a tight rein on Mr. DeBain. I didn't recommend Mr. Bennett go into business with him."

"But he did," Detective Amato said.

"So I've heard," investigator Minot replied.

The two detectives continued to talk to the private investigator for the next half hour as they went through his file on DeBain. They tried to get a lead or a possible person who might be someone to talk to. They were told that when DeBain lived in Kahului on Maui, it was for less than a half year. He could find no reason why DeBain would have moved from Oahu to Maui. Few there remembered him and those who did said he was a loner. "One day a neighbor said he showed up and looked like he had been in a fight. I was unable to find out what may have happened to him. There was no police report. He had a track record of getting in trouble with women and I assumed that the friend of a woman, or possibly the woman herself he had beaten, decided to teach him a lesson. A few weeks later, he left Maui and moved back to Honolulu," Mr. Minot told them. The private investigator found no friends that DeBain made and he couldn't find any trouble he may have had with the law. Unable to get anything positive that would help the two detectives, they thanked the investigator for his time, took the file copy he had given them and the two left. They debated if it would be worth their time and effort to go to Maui and question the people mentioned in the background check, and decided yes. They would need to find out what had happened to DeBain. Who had beaten him and why. It didn't seem to hold out promise but should be followed up on. They believed the private investigator did an in-depth job from what they could see of his report and that they would most likely come up with nothing.

Their next stop was the commercial airlines. If their dead man was going to see land on the main island he most likely would fly. They showed his photograph and had passenger manifests checked and came up with nothing. If he flew from Ohau to Hawaii, there was no record of it.

They talked to charter and private pilots who advertised and got the same results. Detective Amato wanted to continue investigating the possibility that he would fly. "It is possible if he was serious about buying land, a plane might have been sent to pick him up."

"Would mean a trip to Hawaii and checking," replied his partner. "Is it possible that Nikki was wrong? What if he was thrown, or fell, out of an airplane, would easily explain all the bruises."

"Doubt the lieutenant will approve it," said Detective Amato said.

His partner asked, "Has she ever been known to make a mistake?" When he heard his partner, Amato say no, he said, "We should check on private charter boat rentals. It would have been a long trip but it would be possible. He could have gone by boat." They got the same result that they received from the various flight companies. No one remembered DeBain.

Most of the day was gone when the two decided they needed do check on land for sale on the big island. They spent the next hour calling real estate companies on Hawaii. The ones with land for sale had no record that DeBain was an interested buyer, but several of their real estate agents were out. They would check with them when they were in their offices. Unless it was to be an exceptionally big sale none of the people they talked to said they would ever send a plane to pick him up.

They poured over real estate for sale in the papers and called. No record of anyone called DeBain had inquired about their property. If he did want to buy land, they could find no record of it.

At the end of the afternoon the two detectives checked in at the squad room and went to Lieutenant Karawa's office to report on their progress. He looked up from his desk and asked, "Anything helpful from Cole?"

Detective Amato answered him, "He believes it was over the money they had in their business, two hundred and forty K. His inheritance from his step-grandfather."

Detective Malaki said, "Checked with the bank, DeBain withdrew the money about two weeks before he was killed. Came in during the morning, teller remembered him since he wanted it in cash. Told him he would have to come back after lunch, the bank didn't have that much cash on hand, an excuse to allow the bank to check on him. Both she and her manager said he checked out and there was no sign of nervousness and not a mark on him when he picked up the dough. He signed for it, placed it in a small travel bag and left. If it was for the money, someone would have had to know that he withdrew the money. Believe he had it in his office safe. No way working as a bar tender could Cole come up with that kind of dough and his grandfather was a tour guide and ran a small souvenir shop. Had to come from someplace else. The question is, where?"

"Two weeks ago, lot of time passed between then and Tuesday. We wondered why he withdrew the money so long ago? Could he have already bought items from China? Maybe paid someone off," detective Amato said. "Could find no record of anything."

"Forget about where it came from, where did it go and why?" asked the lieutenant.

"Didn't find his cell phone so don't know who he may have called or who may have called him. And DeBain, what a character," said Detective Malaki. "Everyone we've talked to said DeBain spent money like there was no tomorrow. List of restaurants Cole gave us where they would meet said he was a big tipper and that was all that any of them could say about him, plus he would hit on some of the girls serving them. No one seems to know where he got his money, cause most of the time he didn't work. Never came in alone or with anyone other than Cole Bennett. Talked to a private investigator Cole Bennett hired to do a background check on DeBain. Gave us a few names of people that knew DeBain and we checked them out. Nothing. According to the investigator, he was to look at DeBain's past run-ins with the law, any criminal troubles he had, and was there a chance he would be investigated. Something that would affect his partnership. Apparently found several things DeBain had been accused of but nothing was ever proven. DeBain was not a nice person, but he found no evidence that he was dishonest. Only legal trouble was a lawsuit over work DeBain hadn't completed, found guilty of, but later, even that was taken care of and paid off. His problems were of a personal nature and involved abusing women. Nothing else illegal. Gave him an okay to work with. Said he couldn't find anything that said DeBain was dishonest, could be trusted, but advised Cole not to do business with him. Told Cole that he thought that DeBain would steal he ever got the chance. Hard to believe that anyone would want to be a partner with someone with such a checkered past. Either Cole is a very dumb guy, or DeBain really sold him a bill of goods."

"Don't know whose idea it was, but DeBain was looking for investors for his trading company idea. Cole Bennett thought he might be able to help DeBain get the money he needed to get started, not as an investor, but as a partner and their trading business was planned," Detective Amato said. "Their partnership contract said that both names had to be on checks that they would issue. Nothing in their agreement about withdrawing the money from the bank. Since both names were on the account, either could with-draw it."

"Last time he was seen alive was early Monday morning at his lawyer's. No one in the area remembers him walking or getting a ride after he left his lawyer's office. Just didn't see him," added Malaki. "Checked with everyone in the lawyer's building and showed his picture both sides of the street for several blocks, nothing. Both the lawyer and an intern remembered him saying that later that day he was going to Hawaii to look at some land to buy. Checked with all the flying companies and real estate agents and nothing. We even looked at a lot of private listings in various papers. His partner Bennett told us he informed him he wouldn't be able to see him until Thursday because he would be out of Honolulu. I called Bennett and asked if it was possible that DeBain was going to go to the big island to look at a piece of land. Bennett didn't know, but said it was possible."

Lieutenant Karawa was silent for a moment as he thought about all his detectives told him. Detective Amato asked, "How did the governor end up with a half-brother anyway?"

Lieutenant Karawa answered, "Cole and the governor have the same father, Kevin Richards. Seems Kevin knocked up Cole's mother when he was in college. Promises of marriage and she were soon abandoned. Kevin did pay her child support until Cole was eighteen, his father did. Both the father and son acknowledged that Kevin was the father. After college, he married into money and had another son, Bream, who went on to be the youngest governor the state has ever had. What did you find out about Cole?"

"Best we know," Detective Amato said looking at his notes, "Cole took his mother's maiden name, Bennett. She married a restaurant owner who died a couple of years later when Cole was about ten. She tried to run and manage the restaurant but with no experience it was a lost cause. The restaurant had a lot of debt and was lost in a bank foreclosure. She then lived with her dead husband's father until he died. Cole worked in the step-grandfather's souvenir shop and between him and his mother kept the shop going for a while. Couple of years later Cole's mother died. Like the restaurant, the shop had debt and was taken over by the bank. Cole has been on his own ever since.

He's bounced around from one low paying job to another, just making enough to live on."

Detective Malaki said, "We looked for the money but found nothing. When Cole reported it stolen, police techs went over the office and found nothing. All the finger prints they found were DeBain's or Bennett's. Eliminated anyone as a suspect. Not a trace that it was spent on anything. Not even DeBain could go through that much in such a short time and not leave a trail. Went through his office. Couldn't find any bills or people that he may have paid. Searched his apartment, the same, nothing. Cole suggested we talk to Bobby Hee and Doctor Pepper. Both were quite vocal about their strong dislike for DeBain."

Detective Amato told the lieutenant, "Bobby Hee was easy to get information on. Our guys who took the call told us Bobby's sister was slapped around by DeBain. Bobby threatened to kill DeBain if he ever went near his sister again. There was some shoving and pushing. Someone called the police when they began yelling at each other and the fight broke out. One of them took a swing at the other. Our guys didn't know who started it nor could any witnesses say who was to blame. Both were given a warning. Bobby paid for his sister to move to L.A. His manager had arranged for Bobby's band to play Las Vegas for three weeks. A few phone calls verified the manager's statement. Hee's their lead guitarist and the band played every night except Sundays and they are in their third week. On the main land when it happened, couldn't have done it. That leaves us with Cole's other prospect, suggested we talk to Doctor Pepper."

"The incident with the doctor and his daughter drowning. Happened five years or more ago and the doctor was quite vocal in his accusation of DeBain. He would be a prime suspect," and he echoed what Detective Malaki had said earlier to his partner, "but it will come back to the money, always does."

Lieutenant Karawa asked, "Any possibility he was involved in drugs, gambling?"

Detective Malaki answered him, "We will look at both as possibilities, but Cole, the PI and the people that knew DeBain said that he drank some, but to the best of their knowledge, never did drugs, use or sell them and he didn't gamble."

"Is it possible that Cole did it? The police report of it being stolen was to throw an investigation off?" Lieutenant Karawa asked.

"We thought of that and will keep it in mind," Detective Malaki replied and added, "Cole doesn't look like he could do it, would have had to pay someone. We will not dismiss it as a possibility, but I doubt that he did it."

"Have a possible lead. He seemed to have been beaten when he lived on Maui. We will have to track it down and need authorization from you to go there," Detective Amato said.

The following morning it was a quick flight from Honolulu to Kahului, on Maui, and the two detectives checked in with the local police department. The private investigator had told them he was unable to find any evidence that DeBain had been in a fight when a neighbor of DeBain told the PI he appeared beaten. On or about the time the local police had no report of a fight happening. They had no record that Phillipe DeBain had ever been in trouble with the law on the island.

The police department assigned patrolman Kimo to drive them where they needed to go. Their first stop was the apartment complex where DeBain had lived on Maui. When they went to the apartment of Randy White, DeBain's former neighbor, they were informed by his wife that he was at work. She had also seen DeBain, and even though it had been a while, she said, "He did in fact look like he had been in a fight. I remembered that I once heard him complain about a woman, Annabelle, Angelou, Angela, Angi something." She could not provide the detectives with any further information. She said her husband had talked to him on occasion and might be able to provide them with more. Her husband Randy was a fireman and could be found at the local fire house.

While at DeBain's former apartment complex, they knocked on

several doors and asked the few tenants home if they or anyone else knew anything about DeBain, had contact with him. Several said they had seen him on occasion and maybe say hi, but that was the extent of their interaction. None of them had seen the beaten DeBain or knew anyone who had.

Their escort drove them to the fire house where they hopefully would meet up with Randy White. They found him and identified themselves, told him what they wanted to talk about. "I already told the investigator that I saw DeBain and he looked like he was in a fight. I remember he had a bruise on his cheek, maybe an eye that was beginning to look bruised and a cut lip. I commented on what I saw and asked what had happened. He told me his girlfriend and he had gotten into a fight and her brother had hit him."

"He tell you their names?" Detective Amato asked. "Would like to talk to them."

"He never told me their last names. His girlfriend's name was Angelique. No last name. Never mentioned her brother's name."

"You ever see him with the woman," Detective Malaki wanted to know.

Without answering, they saw Mr. White shaking his head no. After a moment, they heard a, "No, can't say that I did. We weren't friends. Only talked to him occasionally."

Back in the police car they asked their driver Kimo if he could look up on his computer if there was a record of any one by the first name Angelique. There turned out to be two, one for disorderly conduct and a second one for prostitution. They believed they could discount the disorderly conduct woman when they saw her arrest was four years ago, and she was sixty-three years old which would make her sixty-seven now. The first name might be promising. It was a long shot but better than nothing Malaki believed. Kimo drove them to the address of twenty-three-year-old Angelique Kia. Her occupation listed her as a cocktail waitress.

Detective Amato knocked on her door a second time when there was no answer to his ringing her door bell. A sleepy voice from inside asked who's there? The two detectives identified themselves and she wanted to see their identification credentials before she would open the door and Kimo standing with them in his uniform convinced her of their authenticity.

When they entered, they saw a messy apartment, a sleepy looking pretty woman who looked like she had just gotten out of bed. She had thrown on a bath robe just barely covering her. Detective Malaki didn't ask her about DeBain, but asked, "Tell us about you and DeBain."

If she was surprised by the statement, she didn't show it. "What do you want to know?"

Detective Malaki immediately answered her, "We are investigating his murder and are talking to anyone who knew him. You need to tell us about the fight you and your brother had with him."

"It wasn't a fight and Trace wasn't my brother," she replied.

"What was it? Witnesses said he looked beaten up," added Detective Amato.

They saw her shaking her head no. "Phillipe accused me of cheating on him! I told him we weren't a couple, he had no rights to me or being faithful to only him. He slapped me! Bruised my cheek and I swung at him and hit him in the eye and forced him out of my place. I showed up at work that night with a bad bruise. One of our bartenders, Trace, asked what happened and I told him."

"Witnesses said he had more than a bruised eye," detective Malaki said. "He was banged up pretty bad. How did that happen?"

Angelique continued. "Phillipe showed up that night at closing time and confronted me. Our bouncer recognized him and admitted him into the club. He said how sorry he was and it was a big misunderstanding. I told him I didn't want to see him again. He grabbed me by the arm and pulled me to him and told me he loved me. I didn't care. We were through. He said he'd never let me go. I tried to pull away from him and he let go with one arm and pulled back to give me a hit. That was when Trace grabbed his arm and pulled it down, grabbed Phillipe by the shirt collar and spun him around. Before Phillipe could do anything, Trace hit him a few times, first in the stomach and then slapped him in the face, hard. Trace is a big man, I think he frightened Phillipe. Told him he ever sees him around he'd put him in the hospital. Threw him out of the place and for good measure kicked him in the ass."

"Did he ever come back?" Detective Amato asked.

"No. He did call though, told me how much he loved me and wanted me to move to Honolulu with him. I hung up on him. Never seen or heard from him again."

"What about Trace? What's his last name and how can we get in touch with him? Need to talk to him," Detective Amato said. "He sweet on you?"

"Last name is Hamilton and you can't get in touch with him and no, he wasn't sweet on me. He is gay. About a week or so after the fight, one of our wealthy gay patrons invited Trace to go an around the world cruise with him on his yacht. Far as I know, Trace did."

Further questioning got them nowhere. Angelique knew of no friends of DeBain. Except for her bar, she knew of no other place that he would hang out. They got in touch with the yacht owner's friends and found out that Trace and he did start off on and extended sailing trip. They wouldn't return for several months.

CHAPTER 5

SHIP AIR HORNS COULD OCCASIONALLY BE HEARD IN A *dingy, dimly lit vacant warehouse near the water front. It had a fifteen-foot-high ceiling and when the last tenant left, he didn't clean up, so it was dirty and cluttered. Dust everywhere. Windows that would be on the second floor, if the place had a second floor, did not allow the sun to come through them, not because they were dirty, but because it was close to noon. The wall with windows had a large loading garage door centered and flanked on both sides with regular hinged doors. These three doors were the only way in and out of the building. In a corner of the warehouse that one of these doors opened into, broken pieces of furniture, a file cabinet with its drawers open and sheets of paper littered the area and said that the former tenant most likely used it as a make-shift office. There were a few empty cardboard boxes and several large stacks of wooden pallets. They formed a wall that would have separated this space from the rest of the warehouse. On this day, the boxes and pallets hid what was beyond it, a bare foot man dressed only in shorts had his arms duct tapped at the wrist to the curved arms of one of the simple office chairs, his legs taped to the legs of the chair. The man was Phillipe DeBain. He was in his mid-thirties, good looking, well-tanned, looked quite fit but not over muscular. Standing next to him was a well-dressed man, tanned and wearing golf gloves, a man unknown to DeBain, a stranger. The white around his eyes said that he wore sunglasses when he was in the sun. He was someone DeBain had never* seen before and didn't know. An inexpensive hard rubber mallet/hammer with a wooden handle was on the floor beside the chair. A leather thong loop was attached to the end of the handle, a hammer that could be picked up at any hardware store. On a broken stool about ten feet away was a portable battery powered tape recorder.

The Unknown Man said to DeBain, "I hear you like the ladies, like to rough them up. Is that true?" he asked.

DeBain was quiet for a moment before he replied in an angry and defiant voice, "Sometimes, only if they want me to. So what!?"

The Unknown Man spoke to him in a soft voice, "I want you to tell me about them." There was no answer and after a moment the Unknown man added, "Tell me what you did to them."

"Nothing to tell, especially to you!" DeBain answered him in the same defiant voice with more anger this time as he struggled to break the tape that held his hands to the arms of the chair.

As if ignoring what was heard from the bound man, the stranger said, "And don't leave anything out."

Again, with disdain in his voice, De Bain spat out the words, "I've been questioned by the police before! You supposed to be someone special!? I'll tell you nothing! You know what that means!?" and he spelled out the word, "N-O-T-H-I-N-G! You got that! No thing!"

"To answer your question, I'm no one special. Just want to hear you talk about the ladies in your life, you can do that, can't you?" When there was no answer, the Unknown Man repeated, "Can't you?" He lifted a two-liter water bottle to his lips and took a drink. He then held the bottle out to DeBain and offered him a drink.

"What's that supposed to do? Make me thirsty then I'll be so grateful I'll talk to you!?" spat out DeBain.

The stranger casually said to the bound man, "No such thing, if you are thirsty I'll give you a drink of water. Here," as he held the bottle to DeBain's lips and tilted it.

DeBain took a drink of water and said, "Now I'm so grateful I'm supposed to tell you anything that you want to know? Well, I got nothing to say, like I said, especially to you."

"No," the Unknown Man said. "I don't want you to tell me anything that you don't want to. First, let me turn on this tape recorder." He turned away from DeBain, stepped to the recorder and pushed the record button. He turned back and looked at DeBain. As he approached him, the Unknown Man put two wads of cotton up his nose and an athletic teeth guard in his mouth. An inexpensive and easy way to alter his voice. He spoke to the man in the chair. "Now, anything that either of us says will be recorded. Do you want to tell me anything Mister DeBain?"

"No! I want my lawyer! Somebody is going to be sued!" said DeBain more defiantly. The Unknown Man didn't know how many times DeBain had been questioned by the police before. He could see that the man he was questioning felt he had nothing to fear. Past experiences told DeBain all he had to do was keep quiet. Out-last this strange policeman asking him questions. The police-man would do nothing to him. They had no proof of anything that he may have done, knew nothing about Darby and her friend. This policeman hadn't accused him of anything. He made no mention of the missing money. This stranger was all bluster, maybe would threaten him, but in the end, do nothing. He wasn't asked if he wanted a lawyer, wasn't read his rights. Hell, he wasn't even arrested or threatened with arrest.

"I believed that you would say that, so I have a message to you from one of your lady friends." The Unknown Man picked up the partial roll of duct tape from the floor near the chair, tore off a piece and placed it over DeBain's mouth, wrapping the tape completely around DeBain's head. Next the stranger picked up the rubber hammer. DeBain's eyes widened with fear. The look on his face told the Unknown Man that DeBain was afraid, that maybe this wasn't going to be an ordinary question and answer interview. Would the police tape you to a chair instead of just handcuff a suspect? Then the Unknown Man could see a relaxed, defiant look on DeBain's face as he moved closer to the bound man. DeBain had put on a self-satisfied face, most likely shook off any potential threat. Then the Unknown Man saw DeBain try to smile. The look said he was confident, nothing was going to happen. Police didn't use force in this day and age. DeBain wanted to tell this stranger, this unknown policeman questioning him, that he wasn't afraid of him and his threats with a hammer. This stranger was just acting tough. What DeBain didn't know was this was not a police-man and he intended to get DeBain to talk, confess about past events in his life. Momentary fear crossed DeBain's face. His questioner was not wearing a tie; could it be that this was not a policeman? Maybe this was someone Pepper had hired, hired to get him to tell the truth about his daughter. Someone else in DeBain's past had the same idea. Mister Oh. But again no. Was it possible that his partner, Cole Bennett, had hired this man to find out what had happened to their money? No, Cole didn't know about the missing money.

He felt confident and self-satisfied just as the Unknown Man asked, "You ever think that what you did hurt?" and he swung the hammer down with great force and smashed the taped man's right foot. DeBain jerked in pain so that he and the chair went over backward. When he and the chair hit the floor, a small cloud of dust rose. A stifled scream could be heard through the tape as tears began to form in DeBain's eyes. He began to breath hard, short deep breaths. The Unknown Man lifted the chair and the man taped to it into an upright position. A pool of blood could be seen as it formed around the smashed foot and mixed with the dust. Skin had been broken and bone pushed through flesh. Not expecting a response from the man taped to the chair, the Unknown Man said in a calm, quiet voice. "I want to hear you tell about some of the women in your life, the ones you liked to beat, wanted to drown. Why you hit them, wanted to drown them. I expect honest answers. You lie to me, I'm going to hurt you. You understand?" Not getting an answer because DeBain was focused on the pain to his foot and the fact that he had tape over his mouth, breathing hard through his nose. The stranger asked the man taped to the chair, "That hurt?" DeBain tried to lift his head to nod yes. Before he could finish his nod the Unknown Man said, "Maybe this will take your mind off it," and he smashed the hammer down on the other foot.

CHAPTER 6

FRIDAY MORNING THE TWO DETECTIVES DROVE TO A RESI-
dential area of town. They drove by nice houses with well-manicured
lawns. They entered a private drive and parked their car in front of
Doctor Pepper's house. A small manicured lawn with flower gardens
flanked the house. From what they could see, a large fence was in
the rear of the house. The middle-aged house keeper, Mrs. Allison,
answered the door when they rang the bell. The two detectives introduced themselves and explained that they needed to talk to Doctor
Pepper. She invited them into the living room and asked them to wait.
The doctor was in the study, and she would inform him of their visit.
They entered a room that was tastefully decorated with expensive furniture. Hanging on the walls were paintings of contemporary artists
that looked expensive, and on the hard wood floor were plush Oriental
carpets with intricate patterns that said money and good taste. There
were several vases with flowers in the room.

Mrs. Allison knocked gently on the study door that led off the
living room, waited a moment then opened it and entered the room.
She closed the door behind her. After a moment, the door opened and
she came back into the living room where the two detectives were
standing. When she closed the study door it did not latch and swung
open several inches. She did not notice that the door was ajar. She

informed the detectives that Doctor Pepper would be with them in a moment. Both detectives declined an offer for something to drink and chose to stand and wait for the doctor. Mrs. Allison said she needed to begin to prepare the doctor's dinner, excused herself and went to the kitchen.

While the detectives waited, they could hear Doctor Pepper on the telephone, "I know you said not to call you. There are a couple of policemen here to talk to me, hope it is not about you, us." He was quiet for a moment, most likely listening to who was on the other end of the telephone line. Detective Malaki took two steps closer to the partially open door. He heard Doctor Pepper continue, "I've sent you the money I promised." Again, he was quiet for a moment before he was heard to say, "No. I don't know how anyone could know." The doctor was quiet for a while and was heard to complete his call when he said, "Goodbye," and the telephone could be heard being hung up. Malaki took several steps away from the door to get closer to his partner.

When the doctor came into the living room, Detective Amato quickly sized him up. He saw a handsome man in his earl fifties with greying hair at his temples, casually dressed and sporting a well-manicured beard. Not muscular, but in good physical shape, the doctor reached out a well-tanned arm to shake the detectives' hands that they offered and in a warm and friendly voice asked, "What can I do for you gentlemen?"

"I am Detective Brian Amato and my partner is Moliki Malaki," he said as he showed the doctor his police badge. "We need to ask you a few questions," he continued.

Doctor Pepper said, "Of course, what about?"

Detective Malaki asked, "What can you tell us about Phillipe DeBain?"

Doctor Pepper spat out the words, "I can tell you, he's a son-of-a-bitch!"

Detective Malaki asked, "Why do you say that?"

"I shouldn't have to tell you! You know what he did to my daughter! Murdered her!" was the doctor's vehement quick answer to the question.

Detective Malaki said, "It was never proven that he did anything. Just your accusation. Both CSI and the ME found nothing that would indicate foul play. Their reports both indicated an accidental drowning."

"He was there! Maybe he didn't drown her but he surely would have seen her struggling or maybe heard her call for help. She didn't have any sort of medical incidence, didn't just put her face down in the water and drown. At the least, he let her die, watched her die!" the doctor blurted out.

"Even your house keeper verified DeBain's explanation of what happened. She was there, witnessed what happened," Detective Amato said.

"So you say," said an angry Doctor Pepper. "She was there after it happened! And the police let him go and he did something to that Oh girl! Read about the girl's grandparents accusing him of foul play. Police should be proud of themselves. They let a killer go so that he could commit another one!"

Detective Amato replied to the doctor's last statement, "The Oh girl was never found. Her disappearance was investigated but nothing was found or could be proven that he did anything to her. It is still believed that she ran away from her family."

Doctor Pepper had no more to say about the Oh girl, so he steeled himself and returned to his daughter and DeBain. He said, "I told Jennifer to stay away from him, he was no good for her. She needed to spend more time swimming. She thought that she was in love, so instead, she elopes with the bastard! A month later she drowns in our pool! An Olympic class swimmer, she drowns! I'd like to take that gold tooth of his and shove it up his ass! He couldn't wait to collect on her insurance, quarter of a million. She never got around to changing her will and it said her money should go to help and support Olympic swimmers. He wanted it, said since they were recently married, she never got around to changing her will, but she intended for him to get it. But, I said, no way. Took him to court to see her wishes were carried out. Judge sided with him, but only for ten percent, because of the short time they were married. Said if she wanted him to get it she would have changed her will. Not much left over after he had to pay his lawyer."

"A small victory," said Brian Amato, "and now he is dead. Someone killed him."

"Murdered!? You catch who did it, thank him for me! Let me know and I'll send him a gift!" the doctor said.

"Help us doctor. Where were you Monday afternoon through Tuesday, from early morning until late at night?' asked Detective Malaki.

The detectives could see that the doctor was thinking about what they wanted to know. Detective Malaki asked him if he was trying to remember or was he thinking up an alibi. Finally, the doctor said, "Monday afternoon consultation meeting with two other doctors concerning a complicated surgery scheduled for Tuesday. After the meeting a quick drink and home by six and in bed by eight. Check with Mrs. Allison. Then on Tuesday, eight hours, plus or minus, on a triple bypass with complications until after five. Eight support staff will confirm that. I cleaned up, changed into street clothes and checked in on the patient. Stuck around the hospital close to an hour to make sure he recovered with no post operation complications, then dinner and drinks with colleagues. Didn't get home till well after nine. Again, you can ask my house keeper what the time was for sure."

"We will check on it. Write a few of your staff names down," Detective Amato said to him as he handed the doctor his note pad.

"Could have hired someone to do it, like before," Detective Malaki said.

"It was just a rumor I hired someone," Doctor Pepper said to the detective. "And you guys picked him up at the airport on an outstanding warrant. I had nothing to do with him, didn't know him and, I didn't hire him! I've moved on. It's been years now."

Detective Malaki looked at him and said, "You did wire money before to an address in Philly."

Doctor Pepper stared back at the detective and said, "A college buddy. I was cleared of any wrong doing. Do me a favor, tell me where the bastard is buried so I can go and dance on his grave, then piss on it!"

"So, you hated him, still do. Who else might have felt the same way, would want to do him harm?" Detective Amato asked.

Doctor Pepper was a little surprised by the question Detective Amato asked him, he replied, "Why? Give me a good reason why I should help you. I prefer to thank whoever did it, not help you catch him."

"You are a good citizen, will make you less a suspect. So, what can you tell us doctor?" Detective Malaki asked.

The detectives could again see Doctor Pepper think about what he had been asked. Finally, after a moment he said, "Jen told me he was afraid of Tony someone or other, over money he owed. Didn't ever say his last name. DeBain owed this guy some money and was afraid of this Tony L."

"Tony L? Ell, was that his last name, like a room addition or the letter?" Detective Malaki quickly asked.

"Tony L, that's all she said. I never asked my daughter his last name. Wanted me to help pay this guy," said Doctor Pepper. "Told my daughter this guy, Tony, would hurt him, possibly put him in the hospital."

"Did you doctor," asked Detective Amato.

Doctor Pepper didn't hesitate, he said, "No! First time I ever fought with my daughter." He was silent for a second and got a faraway look as he thought back on the moment in his life with his daughter. "Remembered her saying that if I loved her, I would help her and her new husband." Again, he was quiet for a moment. In a soft voice, he finally said, "Now I wish I had." His tone quickly changed to one of hate when he said, "I'm glad he is dead! I wish I could have done it! Hoped I could get him on the table with a heart problem, maybe he wouldn't survive the operation!"

"Couldn't help but hear you on the phone a moment ago," detective Malaki said. He paused and continued, "You weren't paying someone money for what he did to DeBain, were you?"

"No! No!" said the doctor.

"Then what was the payoff for?" detective Amato wanted to know.

The two detectives could see Doctor Pepper think about the question he had been asked and how best to answer, if to answer at all. The doctor decided to and confessed, "It's bound to come out if you look hard enough. I'm having an affair with a married nurse. She needs money to settle some debts, and I hope, to pay a lawyer to file for her divorce and then represent her. You can check. I'll give you her name if you keep it quiet."

"We will do both, check with her and keep it quiet if it is true," detective Malaki promised him. "Here is my card. If you can think of anything that might be a help to us, call."

CHAPTER 7

THE UNKNOWN MAN WALKED AROUND THE BOUND DEBAIN. *He still held the hammer and bottle of water. Stifled sobs could be heard through the tape on DeBain's mouth and his breathing was deeper as he tried to come to grips with the pain in his feet. The Unknown Man set the hammer and water bottle down in front of DeBain, took out a pocket knife and opened it. Not sure if DeBain was focused on what he was about to say, the Unknown Man picked up the bottle of water and poured some on DeBain's head. The water got the bound man's attention and he looked up at his torturer. Now, sure he was going to be listened to, DeBain's antagonist said to him, "I'm going to remove the tape, you scream," and he held the knife in front of DeBain's face, "I'll cut out your tongue."*

The Unknown Man walked to the side of DeBain, lifted a corner of the tape and slowly pulled it off, pulling some hair from the back of his neck. The look on DeBain's face told his torturer that it hurt when he slowly pulled the tape from DeBain. He opened his mouth to scream but didn't. His mouth opened wide, a gold front tooth with a diamond embedded in it could be seen by the Unknown Man but he didn't comment on it. DeBain waited a moment so that his heart and breathing could approach normal. The water poured on him began to run from his head, down his face and dripped off his chin and mixed with the blood that began to pool between his two feet. He hesitated, but finally was able to plead, "Please mister, please."

The Unknown Man said to him, "I hear you like to drown women as well as beat them, that true?"

DeBain tried to shake his head from side to side and at the same time uttered, "No, nooo. I would never do anything like that." Phillipe watched the stranger slip his hand through the leather attached to the handle. He looked at the hammer, saw the Unknown Man pick it up and move closer to him. He could not take his eyes off the hammer and his eyes followed it as the Unknown Man's hand went through the leather loop and swung it carelessly. He could see the blood from his smashed feet on the head of the hammer.

"I'll ask again, for the last time." the Unknown Man said. "I want you to tell me the truth, how you like to hurt women, like to drown women? I want you to tell me about her. You don't, I'm going to hurt you, you understand? Hurt you bad, not just like your feet."

"No! No!" DeBain said as he saw the Unknown Man's hand through the leather loop grasp the hammer's handle as he prepared to swing the hammer. DeBain was aware that this was no ordinary policeman, not a policeman at all. As best as he could, DeBain tried to shout as he gasped for air, "Yes! Yes!"

"Yes what?" the Unknown Man asked the terrified DeBain.

"I, I, I, I, like to drown women," the bound man stammered.

The Unknown Man looked down at Phillipe, "How do you like to do it?" he asked.

Since this was no policeman talking to him, DeBain was sure he would continue to beat him and that he meant it, he would cut off his tongue. He thought back to several years ago as he began to talk about his dead wife, sure she was the one this strange man was referring to. After all these years, Doctor Pepper had hired someone to torture him, make him confess, or maybe, kill him. Doctor Pepper could not, would not forget about his dead daughter. DeBain began to speak about her as he recounted the day he killed her, "Jennifer was so pretty and I loved her so much, promised her the moon. Told her I'd do anything for her, anything to make her happy. She meant more to me than life itself." He stopped for a moment and then continued, "But I needed the money. I begged and begged. Get the money from your father I told her. It's not that much and he can afford it, doing two, sometimes as many as one a day heart surgeries a week. Maybe not have the pool fence painted every year." DeBain paused, the throbbing pain in his feet made him wince. He shook off the pain and asked, "Will you let me go if I tell you? Please!" he begged. "Are you going to kill me, please don't kill me, tell the doctor I'm sorry. I let it happen. It was an accident."

The Unknown Man didn't say anything. He looked at the hammer he held, DeBain followed his glance. The message was clear. "Tell me about the accident! How did it happen? Don't leave anything out."

DeBain began breathing harder as he continued to tell about his wife Jennifer, Doctor Pepper's daughter. "I asked, asked her how much he got for each operation. She didn't know or wouldn't tell me. All she could say was, father said no. I blamed her. After we were married she was more interested in swimming than helping me." He stopped and looked pleadingly at his antagonist, tried to ignore the pain in his feet. "She told me she would get a job and help me pay off the debt," and he stopped talking.

"Go on," he heard the Unknown Man encourage him, "continue. Tell me the truth. What and how it happened."

After the pause, DeBain's breathing had returned to near normal. He knew he must continue or maybe another hammer blow to a foot. He struggled to ignore the pain in his feet and he said, "I knew she had an insurance policy, but not how much. Didn't care. Maybe I could get it since we were married. She is going to do a hundred laps. I watch and count. She is in her nineties, tired. I slip into the pool and swim, swim underwater to her. I open my eyes, the chlorine in the water burn them. Makes me more determined. Refused to close my eyes. Swim to the center of the pool. I see her and reach out for her, grab her by the leg. I pull her down. She struggles but cannot break free. No scratches or bruises. At last, she is motionless. I let go of her and quickly swim to the pool's edge and get out. I see her, face down. She is bobbing up and down with the gentle waves of the pool. I run back and forth looking at the water and I yell, loud enough for the house keeper to hear." He stopped for a second and his breath picked up. "Jennifer! Jennifer! I yelled. Then I turn and yell in the direction of the house, Mrs. Allison! Mrs. Allison! I see her in the doorway and I hear her say, what is it? It's Jennifer! Mrs. Allison came from the house and when she is close enough to see the pool, I dive in. I swim to Jennifer, grab her by the arm and pull her to the edge. Mrs. Allison helps me lift her out of the water. I start mouth to mouth. Make sure she is not breathing. I can't feel a pulse and I begin to cry. Between sobs I say oh God, no, no, no. I tell the house keeper to quick call 911." DeBain stopped and looked pleadingly at the Unknown Man. He said to him, "Please mister. Let me go. Please don't hurt me! I didn't mean it, but I was desperate. I needed the money. Tony wouldn't want any excuses. He would send a clear message, hurt me. Tell the doctor I'm sorry, truly sorry. I regret what I did every day and if I could, I would take the day back. I'd let Tony do whatever he wished to me."

The Unknown Man said to DeBain as he stepped to his side, "Now that wasn't so bad. Confession is good for the soul. It will ease your conscience tonight. You'll sleep better. How could you drown her and say you loved her so much, would do anything for her?" The Unknown Man waited for a response, when one was not forthcoming he continued talking to DeBain. "I know you're sorry. People always are after they are caught. Sorry they did something foolish, wish they could take it back, ask for forgiveness. Why didn't you think about what the effect your action would have? Her dead and her father's heart broken. I understand, better for others to suffer rather than you, right. But sometimes circumstances catch up with you and you are sorry. Forgiveness will not be given." And with the final word to DeBain, the hammer came around, missed the arm of the chair and hit him hard in the side of his stomach where his kidney would be. The hammer wielding man took quick steps to the other side, switched hands holding the hammer and again a hard blow to the opposite side of the body, catching DeBain partly in the ribs. DeBain caught his breath. Spit and blood dribbled from his mouth onto his stomach as his head fell forward. His chin on his chest, he struggled to breath. He didn't know much about anatomy but he believed that the hammer blow had broken a rib and pushed it into his lung.

CHAPTER 8

THE TWO DETECTIVES THANKED THE DOCTOR, RETURNED to their car, and drove away. They had decided to check on the doctor's alibi and headed toward the doctor's hospital. Detective Malaki talked about the interview, "The doc may have wanted to do it, but he doesn't have what it took to do to DeBain what we saw."

Detective Amato said in response, "But he looked fit, could have done it, knew where to hit, to make it hurt, make it last without killing him. As a doctor, most likely wouldn't be squeamish about it."

"You're right," said Moliki, "but if it was him, I think he would just get it over, not drag it out. Let's check on his alibi and any money he may have withdrawn, see if there are any irregularities and check on the nurse that he told us about. Find out if he sent her money."

"Are you saying it wasn't for the money?" Detective Amato said to him. "If he did hire someone to do it, it wouldn't be for DeBain's money, he wouldn't have known about it. If he's the successful heart doctor we know he is, surely wouldn't want or need the money. It would be only for revenge." The detective paused for a moment as he thought about what he had just said, and then he asked his partner, "You think Pepper paid someone to do it?"

Detective Malaki said, "Maybe, someone could have been paid to avenge his daughter's death. He could have waited all these years so that everyone would think he had forgotten about DeBain. But you heard him, he hasn't. A lot of hate still there."

Detective Amato responded, "If he did hire someone to kill DeBain, Cole's idea that he gave the money up so the guy would stop beating him would make sense."

"I don't know," said Detective Malaki, if he did hire someone it would be to kill DeBain, not to torture him first. After seeing DeBain in the morgue and hearing what Nikki Collings said, I have to believe that whoever killed him enjoyed the torturing, was a psycho nut case. We will have a close look at Doctor Pepper's finances though."

"Now you believe it wasn't for the money?" Brian asked

All Moliki could say was that they will wait and see where the evidence takes them. After a moment of silence, he added, "We also cannot discount the idea that he was to go to the big island to look at some land. We need to look more into who he may have gone to see about this property."

The hospital interview confirmed everything that the doctor told them about Monday afternoon and Tuesday's operation. Messages they had left about a land sale were mostly returned and proved fruitless. Deciding on their next move, Amato said, "We will go across town and check out this Tony L, the guy Pepper said DeBain was afraid of him. Can only be Tony Locasti."

"Narcotics trying to get something on him for years," Detective Malaki said to his partner. "Maybe DeBain didn't do drugs, but if he worked for Locasti, possible he could have sold them. What if he lost a shipment, couldn't pay for them, what would Locasti do to him?"

"Let's give it a shot, what can it hurt?" Brian said. "Wouldn't be much of a stretch to find out Locasti had it done, accused of having it done in the past. If we believe he had it done, we will have to prove it. If we can't, maybe the investigation will stop with him."

After he thought about what he had said, the detective revised his thinking. "Locasti wouldn't have had him killed, maybe break his thumbs, bust a knee cap as a warning or a lesson," replied Detective Amato. "Let's head over to his place. See if there was some connection between Locasti and DeBain."

After twenty minutes, Detective Amato drove into a private drive that had a closed gate that prevented the two detectives from proceeding. On either side of the gate, a six-foot-high stone wall could be seen. To the left of the gate were a small guard house and a small gate inside of the wall that allowed for the passing of the guard into and from the enclosed area. Detective Amato stopped at the gate.

Out of the guard house an armed guard emerged and approached the police car. Detective Amato opened the driver side window. The guard asked if they needed help. Detective Malaki leaned across his partner, showed the guard his police badge and told him they needed to talk to his boss, Mr. Locasti.

The guard said, "Wait here," and he returned to the guard house. The detectives could see him talk on a telephone and heard what he said. "Five-0 is here, want to talk to the boss." He was quiet for a moment and then said, "Okay, I'll send them in." He looked at the two detectives, gestured with his hand that they should go forward and said to them, "Okay to enter," and the gate began to slide open.

Detective Amato pulled forward and closed the window. He could see the gate close behind him as he looked in the rear-view mirror. "Seems like everyone calls us five-0. Why doesn't the department just accept it? I think it's kind of catchy."

"Not for us to figure out why not. You ever asked to be on the show? Would you do it?" Detective Malaki asked his partner.

"What would it pay?" was his response. Both were quiet for a moment as Detective Amato drove toward the house of Mr. Locasti. "Looks like Locasti is paranoid," he said to his partner, "or maybe just over cautious."

"Maybe just likes his privacy," said his companion Detective Malaki.

After a short drive, they could see an elegant house in front of them. On both sides of the driveway were well groomed lawns, beds of flowers and several fountains. On one of the lawns several peacocks were seen strutting. "Jeez! What a layout!" detective Amato said. "I heard they clip their wings so they can't fly, think that's true Moliki?"

"Don't know. Here's proof that crime does pay," Detective Malaki replied. Then he said, "Drug money can go a long way and provide quite a life style, if you don't get caught."

At the house, Detective Amato parked the car and the two police detectives got out. From the house a good-looking man wearing a sport coat and tie greeted them at the door before they could ring the bell. Amato thought to himself that the slim body and short haircut of the man made him think ex-armed forces. He extended his hand to shake theirs and with his left hand pulled his jacket to the side to reveal a holstered gun. "My name is Mandi, I am Mr. Locasti's assistant and personal body guard. Just so you know, I have a permit to carry. I will need to see some identification." Both detectives introduced themselves and showed their police credentials. Satisfied, Mandi said, "Come in, he will see you now." Mandi led them into a large foyer and said, "Wait here, I'll get him," and he left the room.

Brian said, "Jeez! What a house. I'd be afraid to sit anywhere." The room was trimmed with fine wood and had expensive furniture, plush carpeting and several paintings hung on the walls. Through the windows, they could see the well-cared for yard they saw that flanked the drive and saw that it continued into the side yard with more flower beds and various blossoming shrubs. They could see an Oriental look-ing man with garden tools tending to the flowers in one of the beds. The room and view to the side yard were impressive and the Oriental gardener was responsible for keeping it looking that way.

Tony Locasti came into the room and the detectives introduced themselves. They didn't need to be told who he was. He was a big, well-tanned man and they had seen his picture both in the papers and posted on several bulletin boards in the station. Wearing white shorts, white shirt and tennis shoes, he may be going to play tennis. His warm inviting smile seemed to belie the many crimes he had been accused of. There was no attempt to shake hands. Mr. Locasti approached them and pointedly asked, "What can I do for you detectives? Can I have Mandi get you something to drink?"

Detective Malaki was the first to answer, "No thanks. We are here on official business. Want to talk to you about Phillipe DeBain, your relationship with him."

The look on his face told them Tony Locasti was not sure he heard the name correctly. With a question on his face as well as in his voice, he looked from one detective to the other and he asked, "Who?"

Detective Amato repeated the name, "Phillipe DeBain, one of your, what do you like to call them, associates."

Mr. Locasti had a puzzled look on his face, looked from one to the other of the detectives again and answered, "Never heard of him, got me mixed up with somebody else." Mandi moved close to his boss and whispered into his ear. This time Mr. Locasti said to the two detectives, "My mistake, misspoke, a pain in the ass guy, never dealt with him personally. Mandi says we hired him to do some remodeling work around the pool."

Detective Malaki said, "He was no builder. You sure you didn't hire him to do other things for you, maybe sell drugs?"

Tony Locasti looked insulted and said, "Please. I'm an honest business man. I've never done anything in my life that was dishonest, especially drugs."

"And all the things that you have been accused of," Detective Malaki replied.

Mr. Locasti cut the detective off before he could continue what he had begun to say, "Are just that, accusations, lies. Let's quit the small talk, if this DeBain guy said something about me, that he did something illegal when he worked for me, he is going to have to prove it."

"We have a credible witness that said DeBain owed you money and was afraid of you, and now he is dead," said Detective Malaki. "The ME said, how should I put it, beaten in the Locasti style."

Mr. Locasti didn't say anything but looked at Mandi for help. He was being asked about and accused of something that he had no knowledge of. Mandi spoke to him, "Mr. Locasti, please allow me." He addressed the detectives. "We advanced DeBain almost ten thousand dollars for materials and work he was to do around the pool. He started and after several days, he bailed. No materials ever showed up. Took the money. Bought no material and did no work."

"And you wanted it back or else. Couldn't let this nobody get away with scamming Mr. Locasti. Maybe threatened him," Detective Amato accused.

Detective Malaki followed with, "Maybe break his legs he didn't repay you?"

Mandi continued his explanation of Mr. Locasti's relationship with DeBain, "Mr. Locasti would never do anything like that, and yes, we wanted our money back. I threatened him, not Mr. Locasti, threatened him with a lawsuit and took him to court for the money paid him. It is on file, you can check. He was found guilty."

Detective Amato said, "So he paid you?"

"No," Mandi said. "He had nothing, couldn't pay the judgment against him. That was almost five years ago."

The four men were interrupted by a young pretty woman, also dressed in whites and carried two tennis rackets. She asked her father, Mr. Locasti, "Daddy how soon can we go? We are going to be late for our scheduled play time"

Mr. Locasti indicated the young woman and said, "Detectives, my daughter, Malinda." After several pleasantries Locasti said, "These detectives were asking questions about Phillipe DeBain."

At the mention of his name, Malinda said, "What did that creep do now?"

Detective Amato said, "He has been murdered and we are talking to everyone who knew him."

"What can you tell us about him Miss. Locasti?" asked Detective Malaki.

Malinda said to them with a little anger in her voice, "I introduced my friend Jackie to him when she was here. They talked. She thought he was good looking. He asked her out and they started dating. He quit working for my father but she kept me informed of their relationship. I felt so bad for her, he began to abuse her, slap her around. I begged her to go to the police. I said I'd tell my father, maybe he could do something. She said she loved him wouldn't do either. She refused to see me because of the beatings."

"Why didn't you tell me Malinda?" Mr. Locasti asked his daughter.

She didn't answer her father and was silent until Detective Amato asked, "So, what happened?"

"I felt the beatings were getting so bad, I could hear it in her voice. She showed me her bruised breasts, said he would squeeze them until it hurt. Finally, I reported them to the police," Miss. Locasti said. "They investigated but Jackie refused to accuse him. She wouldn't testify against him if it came to a trial. Then he dumped her and married a doctor's daughter! Seems that he was seeing both at the same time," Miss. Locasti said. "He was a creep and no good."

"Water under the bridge, right," Detective Malaki said.

Malinda didn't reply to the detective's remark for a moment and then said, "Couldn't happen to a nicer guy, won't be missed." She turned and said to her father, "I'll be at the pool dad when you are through talking to these detectives," and she turned and left the room without saying goodbye to the detectives.

"Anything further you can add to what you've told us," Detective Amato asked Mandi.

Mandi said, "Didn't know about Malinda's friend. Shortly after DeBain married the doctor's daughter, he paid Mr. Locasti the money advanced him with interest. Heard he borrowed the money from a loan shark a while after his marriage. I read in the paper his wife drowned. Nothing to do with him or any of that."

"Name of the loan shark?" Malaki asked.

"Not sure, but I'd ask around down at Ben G's," replied Mandi.

"So, you are saying you had no reason to do him harm after repaying you," Detective Amato added.

Mr. Locasti said to the two detectives, "If Mandi says that was what happened, then that was what happened, the way it was. Absolutely no reason to doubt him."

Detective Malaki said, "Maybe you didn't have a reason to kill him, but beside his father in-law, the drowned woman's father, who else you know might want to do him harm? How about your daughter's friend, Jackie? You didn't want to do her a favor, did you?"

Without a moment's hesitation Mr. Locasti answered the detective, "No. Didn't know about her and if I did, would never do anything to him. Like my daughter, would have gone to the police."

From inside the house Malinda was heard when she called to her father.

Mr. Locasti turned in the direction of his daughter's voice and said, "Be right there." He turned to the detectives and said, "My daughter's friend Jackie is happily married and living in Oregon, and according to my daughter, is expecting her second child."

"Could it have been the loan shark?" asked Malaki.

Mandi said, "If DeBain hadn't paid him back, no way would he have waited five years. Five days past the due date would have been more like it. Did hear that DeBain had some sort of trouble with a one eyed Chinese boat owner and his cousin a year or so ago."

Detective Amato took out his note pad and asked, "What is his name?"

Mandi replied, "No name, just a rumor."

Detective Malaki said, "We will check it out."

"Mr. Locasti, maybe we will be back," Detective Amato half promised.

Not in the least bit intimidated Mr. Locasti said to the two, "Any time detectives, any time. Mandi will show you to the door." He turned around and headed in the direction from where his daughter had called.

Mandi said to the two policemen, "Gentlemen, follow me." As he escorted them to the door Mandi said, "Just so you know, DeBain was a loser and a low life. Tony wouldn't have hired him to walk his dog. It was on my recommendation that he was hired on advice from a friend."

"Your friend's name," Detective Amato asked.

"Billy, Billy Lakes," Mandi replied.

The two detectives got in their car. Mandi watched as the car turned around and the detectives drove away. Amato could see in the rear-view mirror Mandi who waited until the car was out about to go out of sight before he went back inside the house.

Driving away, Detective Amato said, "Before we call it a day, let's go to Leo's After Hours bar. Let's stop in and talk to the owner. The investigator got nothing there but he was asking different questions than we will." Like the Parrot's Roost, the bar was away from the hotels and downtown area and catered to local patrons. It was getting late in the afternoon and soon people would begin to drop in for a drink before heading home. Later, the bar would have what would be called a hard-drinking crowd, a lot of them hard drinking navy men. The only décor in the bar was a mirror behind the bottles of liquor and in the back, an old, well-worn and used bumper pool table, two old pin ball machines and a juke box. When they entered the bar, they had to take a moment for their eyes to adjust to the dimness in the place. They went to the bar and introduced themselves to Kenny, the young man tending bar. Detective Amato showed Kenney a picture of DeBain and wanted him to tell them about his habits in the place, someone he may have gotten friendly with. Kenny said he didn't recognize the man since he was the day bar tender and would be getting off work in half an hour. They most likely would need to talk to the people who would be starting in a half hour. They decided to have a soda and would wait for the second shift. They sat at the bar and were served the drinks when Kenny said the two Cokes were on the house. The door opened and a well-endowed young woman entered. Kenny said, "Here comes Angela, an evening worker." He waved her over and introduced her to the two detectives.

She had big breasts and wore a tight low cut halter that barely covered her nipples. Over this she wore an unbuttoned short sleeve shirt that had the tails tied together. She had on her left wrist a Chinese symbol tattoo and wore just enough make-up so that she looked pretty, but most men would not pay much attention to her face. Long dark and curly hair fell past her shoulders.

"We need you to tell us about this man," Amato said as he showed her DeBain's photograph. She leaned over to take a better look and they thought she may pop out of her top. She obviously knew what she was doing and was practicing on these two detectives.

She smiled and said, "Sure, I know him. He used to come in here. His name was Phillipe. I would show him my tits, just like for you, and he would leave me a big tip. But now, he doesn't show up anymore, thank God. Haven't seen him for a while either."

"Why's that?" Detective Moliki asked.

"I went out with him a few times, thought he had a lot of money and he would spend it and show me a good time. He did till he got me in bed. That's when things changed. Boy, did they change!"

"How so? Asked detective Malaki.

"He started to slap me around. Made my lip bleed and he would bite me on my tits. Want to see where he bit me?" as she cupped one of her breasts. "It's been a half year now, but I still have the scar."

"No, that will be alright. We believe you. So, what happened?" Detective Amato asked.

"He bit me so hard I thought he bit it off, my nipple. Had to go to the emergency room at the hospital, three stitches. He begged me to go out with him again, said it was an accident and wouldn't happen again. I said no. Said he got the wrong message from me. Thought I liked it. I told him in no uncertain words, did I ever say or even hint at that I wanted him to hurt me? Couple of nights later Phillipe stopped in. He sounded so sorry and he felt bad that he bit me, I did go home with him. First thing he did was pull at the stitches with his teeth. I stopped him and began to get dressed. That's when he began to slap me around. Well, I came to work with bruises on my cheek and a bruised eye the next night. Our night bouncer, Buddy, asked what happened. I told him and he said I should stay away from Phillipe. Three nights later Phillipe stopped in and wanted me to go with him. I told Phillipe we were through and that I didn't ever want to see him again, he threatened me, said I'd be sorry. Next night when I got off work he accosted me behind the bar's building. Lucky Buddy was there, he grabbed him by the back of his neck, turned him around and threw him against the building. He hit Phillipe once in the stomach doubling him over. Phillipe started to vomit. Buddy lifted his head up and told him he ever comes around here again or bothers me, he would put him in the hospital. Buddy could do it too big and strong as he was. That was a couple of months, maybe a half year ago, or longer, haven't seen or heard from him since. Guess he got Buddy's message."

"You are not going to see him any time soon. DeBain was murdered." He let what he said to be understood by Angela before he asked, "Anyone else here ever have a problem with him?" Detective Malaki wanted to know.

"Not that I know of. I'm the only woman serving drinks and not many women come in here alone. I'm sure when Phillipe sized up any guy with a woman, he would have no thoughts of coming on to one of them. Lot of navy guys who would have no problem putting Phillipe in the hospital"

"He ever talk to anyone else in here. A navy guy who he may have had a beef with? Need to get some background information about him and anyone he talked up would be an interest to us," Detective Amato said.

"Except for me, no one that I could point to. Sorry," she replied. "If that is all I need to put my apron on and get ready for work."

"We will need to talk to Buddy, what's his real name? What time will he begin work? Asked Detective Amato.

"Last name is Moody. Don't know what his first name was. Everyone called him Buddy and he quit, doesn't work here so don't know how to reach him. Same for our night bat tender, Andy. He and our new bouncer, Rick, weren't here when DeBain would come in. Ask Kenny, he might know. Better do it quick before he leaves," Angela told the detectives.

Amato saw the bar tender hanging up his apron so he left Moliki and Angela and walked to the bar, stopped Kenny and asked him about Buddy. "Didn't know him that well because he worked mainly at night and I'm the day guy. Can't tell you how to reach him. I heard about his threat to this guy for roughing up Angela. Shortly after it, Buddy joined the navy and far as I know he's still in San Diego or he's on a ship somewhere."

After Detective Moliki thanked Angela he went to the bar where he heard Kenny tell his partner that Buddy's first name is Mitchell. As they talked the night bar tender and bouncer showed up. Neither could add anything to what Angela said except Rick believed Buddy was on a ship somewhere in the Persian Gulf. They thanked him and left.

When they were driving away from Leo's After Hours bar, Detective Moliki received a phone call from their Lieutenant. One of the real estate agents for Island Estates, a Bobby Leonard called and had information about DeBain. Back at their station Moliki called the number the agent left and put their conversation on speaker phone so that his partner could hear and possibly ask questions. He informed the agent of who he was and what he needed to talk to the agent about. "We have reliable information that he was to see you on Monday and look at a piece of property. Want to know where he was going afterward or people that he was going to meet."

Bobby Leonard turned out to be a woman and not put off by being on speaker phone. She replied to Detective Malaki's request, "He called me Monday morning. Said on the phone he saw photographs of the property and it looked like something he would be interested in. When I suggested a time and place to meet and talk, first thing he wanted to know was the asking price. When I told him, I heard a whistle and then silence. I had to ask if he was still there. He wanted to know if there was any wiggle room on the price. Told him the owner has already reduced the asking price by seven thousand dollars and I doubted it. Thought I'd be honest and up front with him. He thanked me and said he'd have to think about it."

"Did he get back to you?" Detective Amato asked.

She answered, "We never decided upon a meeting and I never heard from him again."

CHAPTER 9

"YOU AWAKE," THE UNKNOWN MAN ASKED AS HE SHOOK *DeBain's shoulder with the hammer. When his question didn't get a response, he put the hammer under DeBain's chin and lifted his head. "Come on, come on, wake up," he said. "It wasn't that bad, could be worse. This water will help." He poured some of the bottled water on DeBain's head. "Water seems to hide your handy work," the Unknown Man said. The water roused DeBain and he opened his eyes. He focused on the hammer his antagonist held. Now that he was conscious of his surroundings and his situation the Unknown Man asked him, "You want to talk?"*

DeBain started to mumble but got the words out, he begged, "Please mister, please let me go. I swear I'll never hurt another woman as long as I live. Please," he pleaded as he dropped his head and would not looked his torturer in the face.

"Are you sure," the stranger asked, "you'll start to think how great it is to touch a woman, how great it would be to run your hands up and down her legs, kiss her, maybe bite her lip. After a while, you might slap her. Squeeze and fondle her breasts, lick them, kiss her nipples, take them in your mouth."

"No! No!" DeBain was able to say as he looked at his torturer. "I don't want to talk about Jackie. I loved her and she left me. Called the police. Same for that bitch Angela and her tattoo. I don't want to think about her, them."

"Tell me about her. What are you doing with her, don't lie," the Unknown Man told him and held the hammer up so that DeBain could see it.

DeBain hesitated but finally said, "Long tanned legs ending at the white bikini bottom line." He stopped what he was saying. The Unknown Man prodded him with the hammer. "No bikini line at her full breasts, Jackie sunbathed topless. I remember, running my hands up and down Jackie's legs. Then to her breasts. I bent down and kiss them. I liked to touch them."

"Who had tanned legs?" the Unknown Man asked.

"Jackie, Angela, no, Jackie had perfect legs," the bound man uttered.

"Go on, tell me about her," the Unknown Man said. "Who had perfect legs, Jackie or Angela?"

"Both," he said "No, Jackie. I, I tell her how beautiful she is, what perfect legs she has." DeBain quits talking about both Jackie and Angela and looks pleadingly at his antagonist. He became less clear as he spoke. He was less precise in his speech. Words were clipped, incomplete and DeBain didn't articulate. "Please do I 'ave to? Don' make me."

'Yes," said the Unknown Man. "Continue, tell me about her."

DeBain hesitated restarting but finally was able to get it out, "I, I, I kneel 'side her, then straddle her. I slap her. I see trickle of blood at corner of mouth. I kiss her and lick the blood." He stopped talking and said, "No! No! I won' tell you anymore."

The Unknown Man is at his side and gently touched DeBain on the shoulder with the hammer. DeBain turned his head and saw it. He heard nothing from his torturer but knew that he must continue. "I tell, tell 'er I love 'er and I kiss 'er breasts. I smear blood from 'er mouth, one breast to other," and again DeBain hesitated and stopped. A tap on the shoulder with the hammer got him talking again. "Angela pulls my head down hard against 'er. Kiss my tits she says and my teeth close on a breast so that I bite her. She yelled and got up. She's bleeding, pretty hard. Took five minutes 'fore it would stop. She tells me it took three stitches. I didn't mean it. It was a acciden'."

"Who are you talking about, Jackie or Angela."

"Angela." He is silent for a moment. "No Jackie. Can't member." He is silent again. "I can't, won' go on."

After a moment of silence, the Unknown Man began to tell his version *of the DeBain's story concerning Jackie or Angela. He continued, "The blood excites you. You can't stop now. Your hands come up to her breasts and you cup them. You bend down and lick a bloody nipple."*

"No! No!" DeBain tried to shout.

The Unknown Man went on, "Oh Jackie, you are so beautiful, like a goddess, such perfect breasts. I want to kiss your breasts; I want to kiss you all over. I love you so much, I want to do nothing but please you." The Unknown Man stopped his narrative about DeBain and Jackie for a moment. He told DeBain, "Here, put your hands over the ends of the chair's arms. Cup them like they are Jackie's breasts, Angela's. Smear the blood over them. Spread your fingers so that you can feel how large they are. How smooth they are. Oh Jackie, yes! Yes!"

There is a moment of silence before the Unknown Man hears, "No! No I won't!" DeBain again replied.

"Close your eyes and remember the feel of her breasts. Do you feel them?" the Unknown Man asked. "You kiss one then the other. You run your tongue over the nipple. You begin to massage them. First one, then the other, then both at the same time. Oh! What is happening? Her nipples are beginning to become firm. They are pushing against the palms of your hands, harder and harder. You take a nipple between your thumb and forefinger and roll it between your fingers as you feel the nipples become firmer and firmer. You run your palms in circles over the nipples. She's as excited as you are!"

DeBain was so caught up in what his antagonist was saying that he didn't see the hammer raised and it came down on his hand, smashing his wrist and fingers. The scream echoed in the empty warehouse. The Unknown Man picked up the partial roll of duct tape and tore off a piece, walked behind the bound man and placed the tape like before, around his head and over his mouth. He walked around to the front and faced the now hard breathing, heart racing bound man. Without saying a word, he swung the hammer hard and smashed the left knee of DeBain.

CHAPTER 10

DETECTIVES MALAKI AND AMATO WERE IN THE LIEU-
tenant's office just before lunch recounting their activities and the progress they had made. "So far, no luck," Detective Amato said. "For a
second we heard what we thought was Doctor Pepper paying someone
off. Instead paying off a married nurse he's having an affair with. She
confirmed everything he said."

"The doc is strong enough to do it himself, but he has a rock-solid
alibi. In a meeting, Monday afternoon, and almost all day in an operat-
ing room with over a half dozen nurses and other doctors on Tuesday."
Detective Malaki said. "Several also said he hung around a couple of
hours after the surgery to check on the patient. No unusual money
withdrawals or transfers except to the nurse. Couldn't find anything
that might lead to him hiring someone to do it."

Detective Amato added, "Pepper is glad he is dead and reminded
us of the Oh girl. The family has moved to we don't know where for
now, but we will find them."

"The doc pointed us in the direction of Tony Locasti," said Malaki.
"DeBain owed him money. Thought it might be over drugs. Checked
it out, it was for work DeBain didn't do for Locasti. Took him to court
and eventually it was settled favorably for Locasti. Eventually repaid
the money advanced him. All of that was almost five years ago. The

law suit the private investigator told us about. It is all in the court's records. The real estate agent he was supposed to meet concerning land he thought of buying claimed he never met with her as soon as he found out what the land owner was asking for it. Checked with a loan shark, Ben Golden at Ben G's bar. Locasti's body guard said he heard he advanced DeBain the money to pay back Locasti. Would cost him maybe ten points a week. Didn't talk to the loan shark himself, in a nursing home. His brother Leland has taken over for him and now is in charge. Wouldn't admit that they loaned money and didn't want to get mixed up in a murder investigation. But as much as told us that if they had loaned DeBain the money, DeBain was sure he could get the money from his dead wife's will and would pay them back in a week or two. Leland said he heard a judge gave DeBain a piece of his wife's insurance and he could pay the money back as soon as the insurance company cut him a check. Everybody was happy. Leland said they wouldn't want to do business ever again with DeBain."

"Any chance the loan shark could have killed DeBain's wife so that he would get her insurance?" Lieutenant Karawa asked.

Detective Malaki replied, "No evidence concerning the doctor's daughter's death that anyone but DeBain was in the pool area and no way that the loan shark could have known about an insurance policy. Doubt seriously that Ben Golden would murder someone for a couple of thousand dollars. Would most likely knee cap DeBain with a promise of more if he didn't pay."

"The information we did get from Locasti's body guard," Detective Amato said, "he was the one who hired DeBain on a friend's recommendation. Tried to check the friend out but found that he died over three years ago. The guard also pointed us in the direction of a one eyed Chinese boat owner. Plan on finding who he is and talk to him next. He's in the investigator's report. Said DeBain worked one cruise for him. No name or address because the investigator never talked to him since he was in jail."

Lieutenant Karawa said, "Before you spend a lot of time checking into his past, check on the most recent activities he's been accused of, ones that may have not made the papers, and keep looking for the money. Who could have taken it? Where and who he has worked for. Check with the stock brokerage company, Shaklee Financial Planner, where he was accused of stealing money last month."

Brian Amato said, "Don't remember reading anything about that. No mention of him from the investigator of stealing money."

"Wasn't in the paper but a report was filed with us. Happened most likely after the back-ground check of him the PI did. Remember the detective Cole hired said he thought DeBain would steal if he got the chance. Apparently, he did. Wasn't publicized, the brokerage company wouldn't press charges. Also, sex crimes reported a hotel receptionist, a Miss. Kayleu, accused him of attacking her on the beach in front of her hotel a couple of nights ago. She can talk and be questioned. Christine Morse doesn't believe you will get much from her. The beaten woman said it was DeBain. Detective Morse's report said, he had a solid alibi. I'll give you her report. Follow up on it."

"She must be the woman his lawyer mentioned," Amato told the lieutenant. "We will look at their report and talk to the financial planner after we see her."

That afternoon the two detectives had lunch at a sandwich shop before going to the hospital where the beaten woman was. They entered the hospital and went to the information desk and found the floor and room number of Danniele Kayleu. They had read the report the two sex crimes detectives had filed and then talked to them and decided to also interview the beaten girl. They wouldn't be able to help with the investigation of who may have attacked her, but she might be able to fill in some of the background of DeBain. They took the elevator to her floor, got off and began to look at room numbers. They reached her room and found the door was open but Brian gave a short knock on the jamb and the two entered.

Detective Malaki introduced the two of them and showed his badge. Make her believe that they are following up on her attack. He said to her, "We need to ask you a few follow up questions about your attack. The original investigators said the guy was masked and you couldn't have seen your attacker but you were sure it was Phillipe DeBain. How could you be so sure?"

From her bed, Danni said in a rough voice, barely above a whisper, "It was him, I know it was. Why can't you arrest him?"

Detective Malaki said to her, "Detectives Morse and Winston said they talked to him and found that he had an alibi for the time you were attacked."

Detective Amato said, "At the movies. Girl remembered him because he made a fuss of some sort over spilled popcorn. Have it on security tape. Went in to the movie and never came back out."

Danni tried to rise when she angrily whispered as loud as she could, "I don't care what you have on tape! I know it was him!"

"Is it possible that he had a friend or paid someone to attack you? What can you tell us about him, maybe old friends, people he knew?" Detective Malaki asked.

She hesitated for a moment and said, "Know nothing about his past or friends. Never met any and he never talked about any. Only went out with him the one time. He took me to dinner at a sea food place, Mama's Fish House. I'd never eaten there and he said it was the first time for him also."

Detective Malaki was writing it down when Amato said, "Miss Kayleu, someone has killed Phillipe DeBain and we are investigating his murder."

Before he could say that anything she could tell them about him might be a help in finding his murderer, Danni showed surprise when said in a raspy voice with a trace of joy, "He's dead! I don't have to be afraid, fear him any longer!"

Detective Amato continued, "Yes, he is dead. You didn't read about him in the paper?"

"No," she replied. "Haven't looked at a paper, spent most of my time sleeping."

"Why are you so sure that it was him?" Detective Amato asked her, hoping that she may say something that would be a help.

She looked at the detective and in a whisper said, "After he beat me, he told me if I went to the police, he'd kill me, that's why. But I did, had him arrested, for all the good it did. Couldn't prove it, but I believed he was stalking me. I was a nervous wreck, always thinking he was after me."

Detective Malaki asked her, "Why do you think he beat you the first time? He have a reason?"

Danni slowly answered him, "After we had dinner he took me home. First time out with him he tried to force himself on me. Never even kissed yet and he is trying to feel me up! Some nerve! He grabbed my breast and I slapped him! He backed away and said he was sorry. I believed him, he sounded so sincere and apologetic. Then he slapped me again and tried to kiss me. I tried to back away from him and he continued to slap me. I was able to free myself from him and ran inside my building and locked the door behind me."

Detective Malaki said, "Initial police report said there was no evidence that you were sexually assaulted, just slapped around a bit."

The excited Danni strained her voice and shouted as best she could, "A bit! I was black and blue on one cheek and had a split lip for almost two weeks! I was so embarrassed I stayed home and missed work."

"His telling the judge it was the result of rough sex that you wanted it plus the lie detector test said he was telling the truth, he was let go," Detective Maliki said.

Danni was silent for a while. She had no answer for what the detective had said to her. Finally, Detective Amato asked, "You have a boyfriend who may have taken matters into his own hands and decided to make DeBain pay for what he did to you? If the police couldn't arrest him, maybe take care of the problem in a different and permanent way. His lawyer claimed that you were fixated on DeBain."

Danni heard what the detective said and in a quieter more con-
trolled whisper that became more intense as she spoke, she said, "Ha!
Fixated! You gotta be kidding!" She was quiet for a moment then said,
"What do you want from me!? I will not help you find out who did this!
And no, I do not have a boyfriend nor am I seeing anyone. I have no
brothers and my father is dead. You need help, ask elsewhere!"

Detective Malaki asked, "Maybe someone is fond of you, but not
romantically. Someone at work, maybe in love with you from afar?
Wanted to do you a favor?"

Danni turned her head to the side and said with determination,
"I'm tired, I have to rest." She hesitated a moment and then demanded,
"Please leave!"

The remainder of the day was spent talking to some of the people
mentioned in the PI report, people who were not home during their
first interviews. They had gotten nothing new on the history of their
murder victim. Both were satisfied that people on the PI's list could not
help filling in any additional background on De Bain nor were able to
give them any new people to talk to or offer a direction that they should
look. If they were asked what they were doing on Monday afternoon
and on Tuesday, they all seemed to have credible alibis.

CHAPTER 11

EVEN THOUGH THE LIEUTENANT SAID THAT THIS CASE WAS important and he wanted it solved as soon as possible, he would not okay overtime work on the weekend. On Monday morning Detective Malaki was seated in Brian Amato's kitchen with Brian's wife Olana. She picked up the pot of coffee from the counter and took it to the table. "You may as well have a cup of coffee Moliki," she said to her husband's partner. "He said he'd be right out, but you know how fussy he can be."

Detective Malaki told her he would have a cup but to go easy on the cream. "I'm trying to lose a few pounds," he said to her. It was not a problem that he would have to wait for Brian to put on a new shirt since he spilled coffee on the one he was wearing. He called the dog to him. As he patted the dog on the side and began to scratch him behind the ears his tail began to wag and it smacked the side of the kitchen cabinet. The more he scratched the dog the faster its tail moved, thumping against the cabinet.

"You do that on purpose, just to have him hit the cabinet with his tail," Olana said to Malaki.

The detective smiled and spoke to the dog, "Looks like Ollie ole boy, is putting on a little weight. Are you boy?" He slowed down scratching the dog's ears and watched the wagging tail slow its movement. Neither his partner nor his partner's wife knew the breed, or how or where the kids came up with the name. All they knew for sure was that it had short hair and was a mixed breed. A rescue dog from the pound. The kids wanted a dog and when after a few years lost interest in the dog, Olana became the one to take care of and feed him. When and if the dog came up in conversation, Brian Amato usually referred to it as the mutt, not Ollie, by the dog's real name.

Olana looked at the dog and said, "It's all the people food Brian and the kids give him. They know they shouldn't but they do it any way. Brian will not admit it but I know he is fond of the dog. Spends a lot of time in the yard playing with him and will occasionally take the dog fishing when he goes. He thinks it's funny how the wild parrot that lives in the neighborhood teases the dog with its squawking and it will occasionally drop things on him. Here," and she pushed the open container of cream to Malaki and continued, "it's half-and-half, pour your own cream." After a moment of silence, she asked, "You dating anyone? Do you ever think of remarrying? Maybe start a family of your own and get a dog?" He didn't answer her but she could see him shake his head no. "You ever hear from your ex-wife?" Again, she could see him shake his head no. He was not upset with the way their marriage spiraled down and ended in divorce. It was a part of his past that he didn't care to visit. And when he did, he came to the realization that the two of them should never have married, they weren't suited for each other. He couldn't say they drifted apart because they were never that close. He had no regrets of the failed marriage. He believed he was too young and not ready for the commitment that marriage demanded.

"Not in my near future. Don't know any women I'd like to spend any time with and I'm not looking. Far as I know, Wendy moved back to South Carolina to be near her parents. They call every so often to tell me they and their daughter are doing well and that is about it."

The two of them were quiet for a moment when she broke the silence. "Brian tells me you caught the DeBain case. He wouldn't tell me much about it. What can you tell me?"

Malaki poured about a teaspoon of cream in the coffee, glad she changed the subject. If it wasn't his partner, then it was his wife trying to get him married again. When she brought up dating and then marriage his thoughts quickly turned to the ME, Nikki Collins. Maybe he should ask her out. He didn't care what she did for a living or that she was a little on the heavy side. The only thing he didn't care for was her bright yellow, almost white, hair. He wondered what its natural color was. He took a sip of coffee, set the cup down and returned to her original question and said, "Nothing. Following up on leads and questioning people that knew him, especially the ones who had a problem with him and we are getting nowhere. Had a lot of enemies, lot of people didn't care for him, even hated him, but so far everyone we've talked to have alibis or they won't help us. General feeling of the people we've talked to is he won't be missed. But, we are just getting started; we will keep digging and eventually will get a suspect."

Olana offered the detective a piece of pecan roll and said to him after he declined, "From what I've read of him in the paper over the years, DeBain was not a very nice man. Ever think of not looking too hard?"

Detective Malaki answered her, "Won't happen. You know your husband better than anyone. He will not want to let it go, plus it's orders from above, we have to solve it."

Brian Amato walked into the kitchen and said, "Okay, let's go."

Malaki finished his coffee, set the cup down on the table thanked Olana and got up. He joined his partner and the two headed for the door and went out to their car. He flipped the car keys to Amato and said to his partner when they were settled in the car, "Where to first?"

Detective Amato said, "Let's check out the stock brokerage company the lieutenant told us about."

Malaki answered with, "Well, head down town."

Detective Amato headed to the center of town and parked close to the bank they intended to visit. Detective Malaki pulled their police identification hang tag from the glove compartment and hung it from the rear-view mirror, they got out, locked the car's doors and walked to the bank and entered. They headed to the bank's receptionist, showed their police badges and explained that they needed to talk to the bank's stocks guy.

The receptionist said, "You mean Mr. Shaklee? He does not work for the bank. He just rents a suite of offices from the bank. He's not in any trouble, is he?"

Detective Amato said, "No. No trouble. We want to talk to him about an employee. So where is his office?" the detective wanted to know.

The receptionist said, "Take the elevator to the fifth floor and turn to your left when you get out. You will see his name on the door."

The two detectives rode the elevator to the fifth floor, got off it and turned left, just as the bank's receptionist said to do. They easily found Shaklee's brokerage suite of offices. They entered and approached the receptionist. They introduced themselves and presented their credentials and told her that they wanted to talk to Mr. Shaklee. She smiled at them, told them she would inform Mr. Shaklee that they wanted to talk to him. "It will just be a moment," she said and picked up her telephone, put it to her ear and pressed a button on the phone. The two heard her say, "Mr. Shaklee, there are two police detectives here who wish to talk to you." She was silent for a moment, replaced the phone and said, "He will be right out."

Through a door that opened into the reception area Mr. Shaklee emerged. They saw a middle-aged man who could stand to lose several pounds, losing his hair and with a jovial smile on his face. As soon as he approached them his hand went out to greet them. As he shook hands with them he introduced himself and heard them say that they were detectives. Pleasantries done, Mr. Shaklee invited them into his office. As they walked he asked, "What can I do for you detectives?"

It wasn't until they were in his office and the door was closed that Mr. Shaklee asked if this was about the money stolen by Phillipe

DeBain. Detective Malaki said, "Need to talk to you about him and the theft."

Mr. Shaklee smiled and said, "Yes, yes. Sit," and he pointed to the chairs in front of his desk, "I'll have my receptionist get you something to drink."

Brian Amato said, "No thanks, we are fine. Need to talk to you about Phillipe DeBain and the money he allegedly stole."

Mr. Shaklee said, "It wasn't allegedly. He stole it! He was a piece of work. Couldn't prove that he stole it or just bad investment advice, but the money disappeared."

"How bad were you hurt?" Detective Malaki asked.

From across the desk they heard Mr. Shaklee say, "Just shy of a thirty thousand. Probably wouldn't have caught him if he hadn't made some inappropriate passes at one of our girls. Groped her and forced himself upon her. Boyfriend wanted to beat him up, instead she threatened to file a harassment suit if I didn't fire him, and so I did. I didn't want to go public with it but I did file a police report and did an audit. That was when we found out what he had done."

Detective Amato's response was, "You must have had some very upset investors."

Mr. Shaklee shook his head from side to side and said, "They didn't know. Reason I didn't press charges it would have been made public and maybe be in the paper. Bad publicity would have followed. Had to maintain our reputation. The company returned all the missing money into their accounts. No one knew."

Detective Amato said, "That must have hurt."

Mr. Shaklee replied, "A little. The company could absorb it, could not absorb bad publicity though. I'm just glad we caught him when we did."

Detective Malaki asked, "Why did you hire him in the first place?"

"That was easy," Shaklee said, "had an opening and he had a business degree."

E. J. STAUFFER

Detective Amato asked, "May we talk to the girl?"

"Of course, I'll tell her you are coming," Shaklee said. "Her name is Charlene Mendez, just down the hall. Name will be on the cubicle."

They shook hands again with Mr. Shaklee, thanked him for his time and went in the direction he indicated. They found her cubicle among the six there and Detective Amato rapped on the side of her cubicle partition and they walked in. Charlene rose form her desk and greeted the two detectives and indicated the two chairs in her cubicle. When she rose, they saw a short woman with a dark complexion, dark hair and a big smile. Like the ME, she was shapely but could stand to lose a few pounds. They declined to sit. "How can I help you detectives?" she asked.

Detective Malaki answered her, "Phillipe DeBain has been killed and we are talking to everyone that knew him, maybe had a problem with him. Your boss told us about you and DeBain so we need you to tell us what happened."

Miss. Mendez said, "Let's go to the lounge and talk." They followed her to the empty lounge area and entered it. She sat, they decided to remain standing. "Don't want my fellow workers to overhear what we are talking about. Too bad he was killed, but I won't shed a tear for him. I don't know if he deserves one."

Detective Amato said to her, "Tell us what happened between the two of you."

Miss. Mendez said, "He made passes at me. I ignored him, thought he was harmless and if I didn't pay attention to him, maybe he'd stop. He didn't. He started making sexual remarks to me and then began to get physical. He thought he was God's gift to women. At first it was just a touch and followed with an, excuse me. But it got worse. One day he grabbed me and kissed me! At first I was shocked, but not so shocked that I didn't respond. I slapped him! I hoped and thought that he got the message and he would leave me alone."

Detective Malaki said, "But then …?"

Miss. Mendez continued, "But then, one evening I was here, working after quitting time. I believed that I was alone. From behind me I
heard him say. Working late Char, or you waiting for me? I stood and
turned toward him. Before I could answer him, he said, come here in a
demanding voice, and he grabbed my arms and pulled me to him. He
held me tight and pushed me against my desk. I couldn't get away. His
hands were on my behind and under my blouse and bra before I knew
what was happening. He smiled at me, that gold tooth of his shining,
and told me that I liked it, didn't I. I screamed at him! No! No! I told him
to stop and let me go! He forced me to kiss him so hard my lips were
pushed against my teeth, hard enough to make one bleed and he licked
his lips. He told me he knew that I liked it and that I wanted more. He
wanted me to tell him that I wanted more and again he kissed me, hard.
I struggled but couldn't free myself. He kept pushing his body harder
and tighter against mine. I was aware that he was getting excited. I
could feel him. Don't know what would have happened to me, how far
he would've gone. But the cleaning staff showed up. I heard a knock
on our outer door and then I heard someone ask is there was anyone
here? We are here to clean the voice said. DeBain let me go and ran
from the room."

"Then what happened?" detective Malaki asked.

Miss. Mendez said, "Nothing, like I said, he ran out and I've never
seen him again. Told Michael what happened and he wanted to beat
him up. He could do it too."

To the last statement detective Malaki asked, "Who is Michael?"

Miss. Mendez answered, "He is my boyfriend."

Detective Amato asked, "What did your boyfriend do?"

Charlene Mendez said, "Nothing."

"But didn't you say he wanted to beat up DeBain?" the detective
asked her.

Miss. Mendez said, "Yes, but I told him no and that is when I went to
Mr. Shaklee. Told him what had happened and showed him the bruises

on my wrists and the bite on my lip. Told him that DeBain created a hostile work environment. I liked my job and wanted to keep it, so I told Mr. Shaklee that I would go to the police and file a harassment suit unless he fired Phillipe, and as best I know, he did."

Detective Malaki asked her, "Do you know what your boyfriend was doing on Monday and Tuesday?"

"Working. Michael's a golf pro at the city's public course and works every day except Mondays," she replied.

"We will want to talk with him. Here," Detective Amato handed her his note pad and pen, "write down his full name."

The two detectives, accompanied by Charlene Mendez, returned to the reception area where they shook hands and left. Mr. Shaklee's office door was partially opened and after he saw Charlene alone he called out to her. She turned and walked into his office.

Later that day the two detectives were reporting to Lieutenant Karawa. Detective Amato said, "The investment company was satisfied that they only had to pay back the money they thought he stole and could keep the whole thing quiet."

Detective Malaki said, "Charlene Mendez, the woman he allegedly groped, had a boyfriend who threatened to beat up DeBain. He didn't work on Monday but spent the day with three friends fishing. Didn't come back to port until dark. On Tuesday, in the morning, her boyfriend had two, hour and a half appointments, one after the other, with two women to help them improve their golf swing. Checked both out and he did. Half an hour lunch break was spent at the club's bar with two or three members and then he ran the golf shop and cart rental until five. Meets Charlene at six or so at a local restaurant for dinner. The restaurant staff verified they were there until after eight. He has a solid alibi."

The lieutenant asked, "What about the girl on the beach?"

Detective Amato answered him, "Either can't or won't help because what he did to her earlier. No boyfriend or family member that could have done it."

"Any luck on finding the money," Lieutenant Karawa asked.

"No, "replied detective Amato. "He was a small-time crook working his way up. Far as we can tell he's someone who liked to hurt women."

Detective Malaki said, "We checked on recent cases where women were beaten and the cases unsolved. Again, nothing."

"Who did he know," Lieutenant Karawa asked, "that he would tell about the money?"

Again, detective Malaki said, "The theft might have nothing to do with the beating. Make us look in the wrong direction."

At this point the lieutenant said, "Find something! I have to report to the chief later this afternoon. I'd like to say we have several leads instead of we have nothing. Keep searching for the Oh family! Check on the boat owner Locasti's assistant told you about. Harbor police may be able to help you. Bring me something!"

CHAPTER 12

THE UNKNOWN MAN AGAIN TAPPED DEBAIN ON THE SHOUL-
der with the hammer and said, "You are a real lady killer, aren't you? Wake up."
DeBain mumbled something that couldn't be understood because of the tape gag
still on his mouth. "What was that?" his torturer again asked. "Don't you like
the ladies?" there was no attempt at an answer from the bound man, DeBain.
He was again prodded with the hammer and the Unknown Man asked, "Like
to kill them? Shake your head." There was no response. He again asked, "Are
you lying?" Still there was nothing from DeBain. After a second he tried to shake
his head a little from side to side. The Unknown Man took the bottle of water to
DeBain and began to pour some of it on his head and asked, "You wouldn't lie to
me, would you?" With that last remark, the Unknown Man removed the tape
and watched the bound man squirm from the pain of the tape being removed.

As soon as he was able, DeBain uttered, "No …! No …! No …!"

"Is that the truth?" the Unknown Man asked.

"Yeth! Yeth!" uttered DeBain as he struggled to get the word yes out.

"Tell me about the ladies you hurt, killed," the Unknown Man told him.

"Wasn't my fault. They asked for it," he slowly responded.

"Who asked for it?" his torturer wanted to know.

After a moment DeBain mumbled, "Charlene. All ever did was kiss 'er an
she had me fired, slut! But I fool 'er an 'er boss. Almost thirty thous. Stupid me.
Could 'av gotten more, but wanted 'er."

"Did you hurt her? Did you kill her?" DeBain was asked.

Slowly he uttered, "No. Should 'av. Tempted me, like a whore."

"Do you like whores, women that act like them? Tell me," the Unknown Man asked as he prodded DeBain with the hammer.

There was a moment of silence before DeBain spoke again, slowly, incomplete words and drawing the words out, "Two 'ore strippers from 'laysia. Could'a twins. Went out 'o their way to pick me up, you hear, they pick me up. Knew I had money. Follow me, follow me out at closing time. Tell me I'm all man, could please bot' of dem." He was silent. His head drooped and his eyes closed. He quit telling his story.

"Tell me, what happened," was met with silence. There was nothing from DeBain. To get him to continue, his smashed right foot was pressed down on with the head of the hammer. DeBain let out a cry of pain, the sharp pain brought him back to life and his condition in the warehouse.

After the pain subsided enough for him to continue, he said, "Took me to dere place. Not even thro door, one of dem began loosen my belt. 'Er han went into my pants an' took hole of me. Led me to their bedroom. She held me while other undressed me. Took my wallet and money. Didn't care. Pushed me down on t'a the bed. They got undressed." DeBain looked at his antagonist and a slight smile crossed his face as he remembered what happened. His voice became clear as he looked directly into the eyes of the Unknown Man, he asked, "Ever been worked on by two shaved whore strippers from Malaysia? They knew what, how to do it. Pushed a small tit in my face, made me kiss it. Kissed, licked and rubbed against me all over. Thought I was going to explode before I finally mounted one of them. Had my hands around her neck while the other kept kissing me. I kissed her back hard and bit her lip. I could taste the blood. She pulled away and yelled something. Don't know if it was meant for me or her friend. I didn't pay any attention to her. The one I was on began to squirm and I went faster and faster. I looked at the woman under me. She moaned then screamed. Then I did explode. The two had quite an act. I pull out and rolled to my side. I never even caught my breath when the second one jumped on me. Took a hole of me and started to rub. Stuck her tits in my face and moved back and forth. One, then the other. 'Fore I knew what was happening I was inside her. She was bouncing up and down, kissing me. I could still taste the blood. Hands were on her tits, then to her throat. I strangled the whore I was screwing." He became silent and his head dropped.

The Unknown Man waited for DeBain to continue. He didn't. It took another prod on the foot in order to get him to continue and his speech was as before, incomplete or incoherent. "Wha, wha," DeBain mumbled.

"What happened next," he was asked.

"Next wha?" DeBain uttered.

"What happened to the other stripper?"

"Wha otter stripper?" DeBain wanted to know.

"You're mumbling, don't make me hurt you. The Malaysian you screwed?" DeBain's torturer asked.

DeBain was silent for a moment before he said, "She jumped off the bed. Saw what did and screamed."

"What did you do?" the Unknown Man asked.

The short break in the telling of the story seemed to have given DeBain the time needed for him to remember and recount what had happened. "The otter 'ore jumped off bed screaming. I 'ump off bed, when after 'er. Grabbed a heavy glass vase. Smacked 'er on back of head. She was dead. Smart enough to wipe ever ting down, poured bleach on the bed and 'ores."

"Why did you do that?" asked the Unknown Man.

DeBain was again silent for a moment before he finally said, "Saw on a TV show. No D an A"

His antagonist was indifferent to what DeBain had said. He asked, "You are still mumbling. Maybe there is something caught in your throat, can't clearly get the words out. I'll help you clear it," and he swung the hammer around and hit DeBain hard on the side of the chest with the hammer, breaking several more ribs.

CHAPTER 13

DETECTIVES AMATO AND MALAKI DROVE DOWN TO THE docks and looked for the lunch stand where they were to meet the two officers they had arranged to talk with. Amato parked their car and the two got out and walked to the lunch stand, saw the two harbor policemen at a table and joined them. They introduced themselves and sat across from the two beat officers. After all ordered lunch, Tim, the older and his partner Bryce, asked the detectives, "What can we do for you detectives?"

Detective Malaki said, "We are looking for a Chinese boat owner with one eye, works with his cousin."

Tim's partner, Bryce, asked, "Why are you looking for him? What did he do?"

Detective Amato said, "Nothing. Right now, all we want to do is talk to him."

Office Tim said, "You must be looking for Wen Hi and his cousin Shen."

"That their first or last names," detective Malaki asked.

"We think it's their first, full name is Wen Hi and Shen Wang," Tim said. "You're too late, won't find them around here."

Detective Amato asked, "Why is that."

Bryce said, "On a tip, about a dozen of us were waiting for him to dock his boat after one of his trips." They were interrupted when the waiter brought them their lunch and there was a break in their conversation as they began to eat. A few moments passed. They continued to talk as they ate.

Tim said between bites of his hot dog, "Caught him red handed smuggling. He was arrested. Currently he is doing a three to five year stretch in the Oahu Community Correction Center. Could have gotten as much as ten years, but he was a first-time offender."

"Cousin got away," Tim's partner added. "We've looked for him, no luck. No one has reported seeing him. We believe he went back to China or maybe California."

Detective Amato wanted to know who the tipster was. The officers didn't know but told him the tip was good and the department has it on tape if he wants to listen to it, he said, "Seems like a small sentence for smuggling, unless it wasn't something like a few small arms or maybe small amounts of drugs," Amato said.

"Neither," Bryce said. "You don't know what he was smuggling, but you want to talk to him?"

"That's right," Amato said, "nothing to do with smuggling. What was he doing anyway?"

Tim answered, "Tell them Bryce."

"People. Illegal aliens. Him and his cousin were smuggling people from anywhere in South East Asia to here. Some were dropped off here on the islands, others he took to California. Everything came out at his trial," said Bryce.

"Not important enough to make the front page, probably why you don't know about Wen Hi or what he was doing," continued Tim. "You want to talk to him you'll need to see him in prison. We believe that his cousin Shen was the brains behind the whole smuggling operation. Lived in San Francisco since he was a kid. Belonged to a Chinese gang until he was sixteen and his family moved to LA. Finished high school there and was sent to college. Speaks both languages like a native and has the smarts to be behind the smuggling. Made money and wasn't as dangerous as drugs or arms."

The detectives and harbor policemen finished eating. They thanked the two police officers, returned to their car and started to leave. Detective Malaki believed they could eliminate the boat owner, but his partner thought differently. He wanted to talk to him anyway. "I want to know what type of a relationship the two had. Wen Hi knew about the money? Since he was a boat owner, may have known about what Cole and DeBain were planning, if they had the start-up money. Maybe DeBain approached him, visited him in prison. Find out if he had contacts in China and could help them." He was silent for a while before he said, "Or, if he had a reason, maybe a grudge against DeBain, could have paid someone to do it."

Detective Malaki asked, "What kind of a reason?"

Detective Amato was quiet for a moment and said, "Don't know unless we ask. Or maybe the cousin did it. Who knows what may have gone on between the three of them?"

"The cousin?" Malaki asked giving it some thought.

"At the least if he worked with DeBain, might be able to point us in a direction we don't know anything about, someone we know nothing about, someone he may have told about the money," his partner said.

Detective Amato didn't have to say anything more; Moliki saw the wisdom in what Brian said. "Let's not tell him DeBain was murdered, see if he brings it up."

"Too late, could have read about it in the paper," Detective Amato answered. "We will just see where our talk to him takes us."

It took almost two hours to get to the center and arrange to see Wen Hi Wang. In a visitor's room the two detectives were talking to Wen Hi. The Chinese man was of medium build, needed a shave and had a telltale scar from the left side of his fore head across his left eye and continued down to the bottom of his chin. His left eye was missing so that the eye lid had grown down and over the eye socket. He answered Detective

Amato's request to tell the two police detectives about DeBain. He didn't use complete sentences or good English but was able to answer their questions. "What you want know 'bout DeBain?"

Detective Amato said, "We heard you had some dealings with him. We are interested in anything you can tell us about you and he, people he may have met, had a disagreement with, what the two of you did."

"Don't leave your cousin out," Detective Malaki added.

Because of the scar on his face, Mr. Wang showed a lopsided half smile when he said, "Maybe DeBain do something 'gainst law. I hope so. They put him in here with me."

"Sounds like you don't like him," Malaki said.

Detective Amato said to the boat owner, "Tell us about him."

Again, the half-smile when Mr. Wang spoke, "I do, what in it for me?"

"Nothing," Detective Amato said, "unless it is something important. Consider it a good deed."

Now Mr. Wang became more serious and said, "You look at him for something. I help you put him away, I do it."

Detective Amato asked, "How'd you meet? Someone tell you about him?"

"No, no," the boat owner replied. "He come look for work. Know what I do. Not bother him. I not know about him and his past. Short a man, so I take him on."

"As a deck hand? Did he know anything about ships? Seems like you were taking a big chance on an unknown guy," Detective Amato said.

"Not work on my type boat but experience on sail boats. He had one when young. Knew the lingo. I say port side he know what I talk about. Wouldn't get sea sick, so I hire him."

"To help smuggle people," Malaki said.

Mr. Wang looked at the detective and answered him, "Yeah. Well, that what I do. First trip pick up family of twelve, grandfather down to seven-year-old. Paid ten thousand each with jewels. I know he have so much, ask for more."

"So, what happened?" asked Detective Amato.

Wen Hi answered him, "Second day out, grandfather complain to me, one of crew touching his women."

Detective Malaki wanted to know, "What did you do about it?"

Wen Hi said, "Nothing. It happen before."

Detective Amato was hoping that he would get something import-ant from the boat owner and he said, "But then ..."

"Yes, but then," Wen Ki said, "almost in port and old man missing. I search boat and found one of granddaughters in a cabin tied to bed, beaten and gagged. I don't ask DeBain, I 'cuse him. He tell me she wanted tied up and got little out of hand. She no talk good English so not tell what DeBain said. Tell me in Chinese what happened and who did it. Tell DeBain, stay away from women. Last time he work for me."

"What about the grandfather?" asked Detective Malaki.

"Never find old man," answered Wen Hi. "Put girl in boat, dropped her and others on shore and made port. Who she tell what happen, who beat her, who brought her here?"

Detective Malaki wanted to know about his missing grandfather and asked, "The grandfather ever found?"

Mr. Wang said, "Never find him. Maybe old man slip, fall over board. Happen before. Calm sailing, no rough water, not likely. Thought DeBain push over-board, not sure."

Detective Amato asked, "That why the bad blood?"

Mr. Wang said, "Never think about it. Too bad for old man. I take jewels to fence I know, he tells me guy named DeBain also sell him jewel stones, cheap. It all come together. I look for him. He afraid of me. He tell police where I be. Get caught. Lose eye in fight ten year ago." That funny half smile of the boat owner returned when he said, "Put DeBain here with me, lose other eye."

Detective Amato said, "You don't have to worry about him or expect him to be sent here. He has been murdered."

The boat owner's smile got a little bigger. Both the detectives looked at him. Mr. Wang asked, "Why you look at me? I do it, I drop him in very deep water, you never find body."

Detective Malaki asked, "Just out of curiosity, did you have any wooden chairs on your boat?"

Wen Hi looked at the detective with a question written on his face, "Why you ask?" The detective didn't answer, Wen Hi finally said, "No wood chairs, metal or stools."

Detective Amato said, "Can't find your cousin by the way."

Wen Hi smiled again and answered the detective, "Moved back to China. Get good job as interp. He speak very good English. Know lot about how Americans think and act. Easy someone hire him."

"Or maybe he moved to California and doing the same thing," Detective Amato said.

Again, the lop-sided half smile, "Could be so, not sure. You have difficult finding. All look the same to you."

The two detectives found where Wen Hi's boat was impounded and stored. A quick but careful inspection turned up nothing that would suggest that DeBain was beaten on the boat.

CHAPTER 14

THE UNKNOWN MAN TOOK A STEP CLOSER TO DEBAIN AND *tapped him on the shoulder with the hammer. "Wake up, wake up." When he could see that DeBain had heard him, the Unknown Man asked, "That hurt?" When there was no answer he poked DeBain on the side close to where he had hit him. He could see a broken rib partially coming through broken skin and a trace of blood. The new taps where the bruise was forming got DeBain's attention. A low audible moan was heard. The Unknown Man was sure that he could smell urine. He asked, "You piss yourself?" DeBain tried to answer his torturer, but his chest was heaving. He had trouble breathing. Except for the moan, he was quiet. Tears could be seen running down his cheeks, mixed with the blood and spittle that dribbled from his mouth. The blow to the ribs most likely also pushed a broken rib into his lung. He struggled to get the words out but they were slurred and difficult to understand. The Unknown Man placed the head of the hammer under the beaten man's chin and lifted the head. He looked him straight in the eye and said, "That right? Pissed yourself?" There was no answer. He waited a moment and said, "Quit crying. Be a man." DeBain tried to gain control of himself and looked back at his antagonist. The tears stopped and his breathing became more even. The Unknown Man waited while DeBain coughed and tried to clear his throat. After a moment passed, he told DeBain, "Forget about the piss. Tell me about the woman you beat. You liked hurting her, didn't you? Make it last, not like the stripper. You liked*

109

feeling her tits? But maybe they weren't as big as Jackie's or big as Angela's. Do you prefer small ones instead? Like the stripper's?" There was no response from the bound man so the Unknown Man bumped DeBain's chin with the hammer and repeated the question, "Do you like small ones better?" DeBain did not try to speak but began to shake his head no. "Are you shaking your head no? Do you really mean no? What? I can't hear you."

Finally, DeBain was able to speak, "No ... No ... No ..."

"No? No, what?" asked the Unknown Man. He waited for an answer, didn't get one so he continued, "You didn't want to feel her breasts? You didn't think they would feel nice? Maybe kiss them, take her nipple into your mouth, rub it with your tongue, nibble on it." DeBain gave his head a slight shake to the left and right to say no when the Unknown Man asked, "What kind of a man are you anyway. You're not one of those guys who think more than a mouthful is wasted are you?"

Both men were silent for a moment when DeBain said, "No."

His torturer said, "No what?" and he gestured with the hammer.

DeBain tried to clear his head. He tried to speak but again his words were not complete and his sentences not finished, he said, "Okay, okay I like 'mall 'its too."

The Unknown Man gestured to him with the hammer and said, "That's more like it. Tell me about the girl with the small breasts. Like the strippers, don't leave anything out."

"No," DeBain was barely able to utter. He was threatened with the hammer. "Okay, Okay, don' 'it me." He appeared to take a deep breath, his head down, he blurted. "I grabbed 'er from behin', I push 'er down, my hand over 'er mouth. I gagged 'er. I 'lipped a belt 'round one wris and tied 'er to the cabin's bunk bed, then other wris. She squirmed but could' get free. I straddle 'er and ripped off 'er blouse." He was silent. The Unknown Man pushed down on one of DeBain's smashed feet with the hammer. DeBain let out a quiet scream. He stopped the scream and mumbled. "I kissed her tit through 'er bra. You like that I ask 'er. Tell you like that. I yell to 'er. She quiet," and so was DeBain. The Unknown Man waited but there was no response from the bound man. He

poked the smashed ribs with the handle of the hammer. The sharp pain elicited a response from De Bain. "She, she couldn't answer me. I pull 'er bra until it tore free." He looked pleadingly at the man holding the hammer, "Pleath Mis'er, pleath don' 'it me."

DeBain's torturer held the hammer in a threatening position and said, "Go on! Continue! Tell me about the girl with small breasts!"

"No, no," said DeBain. He was encouraged to continue with another sharp jab to the bruise on his chest. After the short-lived yell and his ability to breathe he said, "I kissed 'er bare breasts, one ten ta other. I bit one, made it bleed. I tole 'er she my yellow skinned beauty. Tole 'er, tell me liked it. No answer through gag. I slapped 'er, then again. I cup 'er breasts and squeeze." He went silent.

The Unknown Man said, "You cup her breasts, one then the other. You kiss them again, maybe smear the blood around. It's small enough to take into your mouth. You rub the nipple with your tongue. She probably liked that."

"Yeth, yeth," said DeBain. "Tole 'er she tell, I kill 'er and all of 'er family. You un'erstan', I ask 'er? Shake your head yes. No! She doesn't un'erstan'. This'll teach you. I slap 'er again and again, harder."

"You like it, don't you Mr. DeBain," the Unknown Man said. "Shake your head yes."

"Yes. Yes," DeBain said and then realized what he was saying and gave out a loud, "No! No!" as the hammer came down on his other wrist. His scream echoed in the empty warehouse.

CHAPTER 15

THAT AFTERNOON AND THE TALK WITH WEN HI WANG, THE two detectives were in the lieutenant's office reporting on the progress they had made. Detective Amato told the lieutenant that everyone they had talked to, either were innocent or had an alibi. So far, they had gotten nowhere, had checked all their leads and did not have a suspect.

Lieutenant Karawa said, "I'm getting calls from the chief. He wants to give the governor some answers. You didn't get anything from the girl on the beach, check out some of the people she knows, works with. Somebody did it and they had a reason. If it was over his treatment of women it could possibly tie into the last girl beaten. She said it was DeBain. Re-interview the people you've talked to. Pressure people if you must. I still think it's going to come back to the money. Find it!"

The two detectives could plainly see that the lieutenant was serious and not pleased with the lack of progress they had made. After they left the lieutenant's office, Amato thought that the lieutenant must really be getting pressure from the chief. Detective Malaki suggested they talk to Danielle's hotel associates. He had read Detectives Morse and Winstin interview of the hotel staff and that they had gotten nowhere. He told his partner he thought that maybe someone she worked with might provide a clue. When they asked several people at the hotel who Danielle was friendly with, which of the other hotel female staff she might have befriended, talked to, the name that came up the most often was Raymond Lakaa.

They found him carrying a wind surfer back to the store room. They approached him, showed their identification and told him they wanted to talk to him. They had some questions about the beaten hotel girl, Miss. Kayleu, and the guy she accused of assaulting her. "Is there somewhere we can go that is not so public," Detective Malaki asked.

Raymond said, "Yes, not many people at the pool this time of day, we can sit at a table." The detectives followed Raymond to the pool as he wove his way past the few people at tables and chairs to a table at the far end of the pool shaded by palm trees, away from everyone. He indicated a table, pulled a chair from the table and said, "If you'd like, I can get us all a drink." The detectives declined and sat.

Detective Amato asked, "You were Miss. Kayleu's friend? Brought her flowers at the hospital?"

"Yes," Raymond said. "What does that have to do with her beating?"

Detective Malaki said, "Please let us ask the questions, you just answer them." He would be the bad cop at this interview.

Amato asked, "How long have you known her?"

"What does ...," Raymond began to ask when Detective Malaki loudly cleared his throat. Raymond did not finish the question he was about to ask, when he turned and looked at the detective. Raymond might not be the smartest man on the island but he knew the detectives were serious about questioning him, and not just about the beating. He decided to answer only the questions asked. "Ever since she began working here. About three years or so."

"You like her?" Malaki asked. "Do anything for her? Maybe date her? Take her flowers at the hospital?"

He answered, "Yes, I liked her. No, I never dated her and yes, I took her flowers. She worked here!" he said as he got angry at the questions and their implications that he and Danielle possibly had an affair.

Before Raymond had the time to get back in control Detective

Amato said, "I saw her in the hospital. Such a pretty girl and beaten for no good reason."

Raymond said, "I'd like to get a hold of the guy that beat her, I'd sure fix him so that he'd never beat anyone again!"

Detective Malaki said, "You're big and strong. You could really do a number on him."

"Probably put him in the hospital," Detective Amato added.

"You know the guy she accused, Phillipe DeBain, was murdered. Did you do it!?" demanded Malaki. "Did you find DeBain and beat him!? Kill him!? Did you!? Did you do it for Danni!?"

Just as strongly as he was accused, Raymond answered just as sure of himself, "No! Absolutely not!"

"Where were you on Monday and Tuesday?" Detective Malaki asked. "All day? Start from when you got up in the morning."

Raymond calmed down and could answer the question, "Clocked in at eight and set up tables and chairs and skim the pool until about ten, both days. Ask the receptionist. Then I took an early lunch in our restaurant reserved for hotel staff, both mornings. Monday I worked late setting up for a wedding banquet at the hotel. In the afternoon on Tuesday I taught wind surfing to several families and got home around eight. You can check."

"We will," said Amato. "Here," and he handed his note pad and pen to Raymond, "write down the names of the families you worked with." Then Detective Amato in a more relaxed tone that said he believed what Raymond had just told them asked, "Who did she date? You ever see her with anyone? We were told that you were close to her. Overly friendly. Probably someone she trusted, maybe confide in. She ever date anyone beside this guy DeBain? Maybe one of the hotel guests?"

Raymond said, "Yes, I was close to her as well as everyone else who worked here. We are all close. And no, as far as I know she never dated anyone. Stayed pretty much by herself. Only one I knew about was DeBain and what he did the first time."

Detective Malaki said, "You sure? A pretty girl like her?"

"How did she meet him?" Detective Amato asked.

Raymond looked at the detective and answered, "Don't know. She never told me and I never asked. None of my business."

"Still, a pretty girl like that, had to have guys hit on her, maybe ask her out," Detective Malaki said.

Raymond shook his head and said, "If she was seeing anyone I sure didn't know about it. She was friendly with all our guests, which was why they made her a receptionist. There is one of our guests you might want to talk with though."

"Who," Amato wanted to know.

"I know that he walked her home one night," replied Raymond. "Other than that one time, I never seen them together and never heard her talk about him. He's a nice guy, couldn't have done it."

Detective Amato again handed Raymond his note pad and said, "Here, write down his name. Let us decide if he's a nice guy and couldn't have done it. I'll leave a message with the desk that we need to talk to him."

They thanked him for his time and said if anything else comes to mind, give them a call. Detective Malaki handed Raymond his card, "Here's my card, call me."

Later that afternoon it was almost quitting time, in the police interview room, the two detectives were talking to the hotel guest Raymond told them about, Benjamin Knight. They thanked him for coming to the police station but told him they gladly would have gone to the hotel and talk to him. He told the detectives that he was doing some sightseeing of the city, so it was no problem and then said, "The message I received said that you were talking to just about everyone at the hotel about the attack of Danni on the hotel's beach and you wanted to talk to me."

Detective Malaki said, "That's right. How well did you know her?"

Mr. Knight didn't hesitate to answer, "Not very well. She is the hotel receptionist and arranged for me to do some touristy things here."

Detective Malaki followed up with, "You call her Danni. Why? You two were close?"

"No," replied Mr. Knight. "Her name tag said Danni, never heard anyone call her anything else."

Detective Brian Amato asked in a friendly voice, "How long you been here?"

"Into my second week," replied Knight.

"Long vacation," Detective Malaki said to him.

Mr. Knight ignored the last comment and asked the two policemen how he could help them.

Detective Malaki said, "We got a witness said you dated her. You weren't trying to avenge her getting beaten by going after the guy she accused. Maybe gave him a dose of his own medicine."

Mr. Knight said, "I read the dead guy was beaten, means he probably got in a few licks. You see a mark anywhere on me?" He looked directly at Detective Malaki and said, "If you want, I'll take off my shirt for you detective."

"No, No, Mr. Knight. That won't be necessary," Detective Amato answered him.

"Why are you here Mr. Knight?" Malaki asked. Not waiting for an answer, he quickly added, "You are by yourself. No one has ever seen you with a woman since you've been here. Why is that? You gay?"

Knight wasn't pleased with the direction the questions he was asked were going and he snapped back to the detective, "Why!? You want a date!?"

Detective Malaki got up out of his seat and in a threatening pose shot back at the hotel guest, "Don't crack wise with me!"

Mr. Knight, smiling, shot right back, "Don't ask me out in a roundabout way, you want a date, just ask. I don't see a ring on your finger. You must be single. Your partner will understand."

Detective Amato saw his partner glower at the man they were interviewing and thought the interview might get out of hand so he told his partner to sit and he turned his attention to why the hotel guest was here and said, "Both of you, calm down." He decided to be politer and after a moment he resumed questioning Mr. Knight, "Just answer the questions sir."

"Sure," said Knight, 'I'm here to rest and recover. My boss' idea"

"Recover from what," Detective Malaki asked.

Still a little bit peeved at detective Malaki, Mr. Knight said, "It's really none of your business but I'll tell you. I was shot in the Mid-East, twice. Once in the leg and again in the lung."

"You in the military," asked Detective Amato.

Knight replied, "Was once, but not now. An analyst and consultant for the government when I was shot. I'm here on its nickel."

Detective Malaki still wanted to somehow get even for Knight's remarks about him wanting a date asked, "Why can't we find an address for you back in the states? The hotel sign in book just has your address as Richmond, Virginia."

Knight replied, "None of us are listed, for our own protection." He couldn't let go of the short antagonistic exchange of words he and the detective had when he answered, "Why? You thinking of writing me later? Want an address? Maybe a phone number?"

Brian Amato tried to keep the questions on point, away from his partner when he quickly asked, "You do have one though?"

Knight knew the game the two detectives were playing, so he decided to be civil to one and not so the other when he answered the question, "You need to know, I'll give you a telephone number to call. Ask for Josh, identify yourself and if you have clearance, he will tell you what you want to know."

"We need clearance? You involved in a lot of secret hush-hush stuff," Detective Malaki snapped.

Mr. Knight looked at Malaki and said, "Yes. A lot of secret hush-hush, secret stuff." He turned his attention to detective Amato and asked him, "What do you want to talk to me about."

Detective Malaki was quick to respond before his partner could say anything, "You dating Danielle, the girl beaten on the beach! Beating up her attacker!"

Knight looked Detective Malaki in the eye and said, "Where do you guys get your information? Are you sure you are the police?" To rile Detective Malaki, he said, "Before I answer any more questions, I need to see your badges again, if not, I'm leaving! If you are two of Honolulu's best, I'd sure hate to meet its worst."

"I told you to quit cracking wise with us!" shot Detective Malaki.

To irritate Malaki further Knight didn't say anything. After a moment, he said, "Well, I'm waiting."

"You serious?" Detective Amato asked.

Knight didn't do or say anything, just waited silently. Detective Amato knew that the man they were interviewing was serious. He wanted to upset Malaki and would keep quiet until the two detectives complied with his demand. To keep the interview moving along he removed his badge and held it out to Knight. Knight glanced at it and shook his head okay. He turned and looked at Malaki. The detective was getting madder by the moment and hesitated. Knight began to drum his fingers on the table to show his impatience with the detective. Finally, Malaki took out his badge and showed it to Knight. Before he could put it away, Knight reached out and took it. He studied it for a moment then flipped it over to look at the picture of the detective with its information and description of the detective. He slowly read it and studied the picture and looked back and forth from the picture and to the detective. Malaki grabbed his badge and put it away. Knight just smiled at the detective and turned and looked at Amato.

Detective Amato again resumed control of the interview and would attempt to run the remainder of it when he said, "All we want to do is clear this up and maybe you can help. Tell me about you and her."

"Nothing to tell," the hotel guest said. "After a pig roast at the hotel, she asked me if I'd escort her home."

Malaki had to jump in and was quick to respond, "Thought you were going to get lucky?"

Knight ignored him and continued, "Told me she didn't want to be out alone after dark. Thought someone might have been stalking her and she was quite clear and positive that the police couldn't protect her." He looked directly at Detective Malaki and said, "That true? You couldn't protect her?" It was a question as well as a statement. When there was no response he answered detective Amato's question, "Only time I was ever alone with her."

In a calm voice detective Amato asked, "Why you? Why not another hotel employee, or a taxi?"

. Knight answered, "I don't know. You have to ask her."

Amato continued, "Then what happened?"

The detectives could see that Mr. Knight was thinking back to the night and said, "It was a nice night. She told me she lived about a mile and a half from the hotel so we decided to walk. I said good night at her door. Stopped at a fruit store and had a fruit bowl and then walked back to the hotel."

"You spend the night with her!" Detective Malaki asked. "Anyone verify you didn't beside you and her!?"

Without turning and looking at the detective, Mr. Knight answered his accusation, "Talk to the owner of the fruit store near where she lives. Stayed and talked to the owner about football until closing time, about, one. Check with him."

Detective Malaki said, "We will!"

"Then what did you do?" Detective Amato asked.

"Walked back to the hotel, lobby cameras should show you the time," replied Knight.

Detective Malaki asked, "Where were you last Monday?"

Knight answered, "Danni," and he stressed her name, "had arranged an all-day tour to your highest mountain, Mauna Kea and then sightseeing past some of the hotels on Hawaii. Flew to the big island and flew back to Ohau and my hotel about nine o'clock or so.

"How about Tuesday?" asked Detective Amato.

Knight made a show of trying to remember and said, "Signed up for day tour with the hotel. Left about six. Back to Hawaii. First, a pineapple growing field and processing plant. Then see a live volcano and visit the Pearl Harbor Memorial in the afternoon. Check with the tour company."

"We will," said Malaki.

Tuesday morning, they reported in to the lieutenant, Detective Amato told him they talked to everyone again. This time they talked to the beaten girl's neighbors, people that knew her and hotel guests. They talked to everyone that knew DeBain, and nothing. Malaki said, "It's all there in our report."

"We thought that we had a suspect, Ben Knight, a hotel guest," Detective Amato said. "He was seen with the girl, and no one could remember him being on a tour on Tuesday afternoon that he told us about. But he wasn't the only one missing. At least until we talked to two English tourists that no one else remembered. Seems like the three of them hooked up and instead of going to the Memorial in the afternoon, they go to a bar. According to the bar tender they stayed until closing time and he poured them into a cab. One of the guys didn't remember this guy Knight at all until his buddy asked if we meant this chap Benny. Yeah, he told us, Benjamin Knight, because that was how we referred to him, Mr. Knight. Then it all came together. They never heard his last name and called him Benny. Can rule him out. We are getting nowhere."

Detective Malaki said, "Spending a lot of time and talked to a lot of people, they may have had a reason to kill him but they all have solid alibis.

Lieutenant Karawa said, "There is nothing in your report about the Oh family."

Amato replied, "We haven't looked that hard yet, but we couldn't find them."

"About a year ago," the lieutenant said, "the family filed a missing person report. The grandfather said that DeBain killed his granddaughter."

Brian Amato said, "Yeah, barely remember it. Doctor Pepper also mentioned it"

"I did some looking for you," the lieutenant said. The police on Oahu reported that they moved to Lanai about half a year ago, Mrs. Oh's parents old place. Take a boat ride and talk to them. Then I want you to check out any open cases of men who were beaten."

They arranged a boat ride to Lanai island that afternoon and the two detectives met Mr. Thomas Oh senior on his patio. He was easily in his mid-sixties with white hair. They showed their credentials and told him that they wished to talk to him about his missing granddaughter. He invited them into his house but they said that it was a nice day, not too hot and they could talk on the patio. He wanted to get the two detectives something to drink but they both declined. When Mr. Oh joined the two at his patio table they all sat and Detective Amato said, "So, tell us, what happened?"

Mr. Oh said, "He killed her! That is what happened."

Detective Malaki asked, "Who killed her?"

"DeBain!" Mr. Oh said. "Phillipe DeBain killed her!"

At the mention of DeBain's name, Mr. Oh's wife, Willa, came out onto the patio. A small woman with greying hair sat next to her husband and took hold of his hand. The two detectives both stood and greeted her. After introductions were over they all again sat and Mr. Oh said to his wife, "They are following up on Connie's death."

"Good," Mrs. Oh said, "you've found something."

"No," Detective Malaki said, "and there is no proof that she is dead. How do you know DeBain killed her?"

Mr. Oh said, "We lived on Ohau then, my wife Willa, my grandson Thomas the third and our granddaughter Connie. My son and his wife were killed in a boating accident. Our two grandchildren moved in with us and became like our own children."

Willa reached across the table with a picture and said, "Here is a picture of her. She was a pretty girl but shy."

Mr. Oh said, "Then that son-of-a-bitch, sorry mother," he said as he looked at his wife, "came along."

Willa Oh continued to tell about their granddaughter, "Connie was working as a hostess on an evening cruise with dinner around Oahu. How she met him I don't know, but he swept her off her feet. The first guy in her life, she was in love."

Mr. Oh said, "The first time she came home with a bruise on her cheek ..."

Willa angrily said, "We knew he had hit her!"

Mr. Oh said, "She denied it of course ..."

"Fell against a booth bench on the boat she told us," Willa said.

"She wouldn't listen to us," Mr. Oh said. "The more we tied to warn her to stay away from him, the more she went to him. She didn't care that he was accused of drowning his wife. She knew him, could see into his soul. Ha!"

Willa Oh said, "She wouldn't come home sometimes at night."

"We knew that she was sleeping with the bastard!" Mr. Oh said. "Sorry mother."

"Don't apologize, I call him worse in my mind," his wife said.

Detective Malaki asked, "What happened?"

Mrs. Oh said, "After a while we hoped for the best for her, maybe their romance would work out for the better."

Then with sadness in his voice instead of the anger Mr. Oh had been using, he said, "Then she came home with something torn in her shoulder." Just as soon as his tone had softened anger returned when he said, "A strap held her arm to her side in a sling!"

"Father wanted to call the police," Willa said. "She broke down and cried. Begged us not to involve the police."

"Shouldn't have listened to her," Mr. Oh said. "Next day she was gone. We knew, back to him."

"When she didn't come home after a week we sent our grandson to look for her at DeBain's place," Mrs. Oh said.

"DeBain told our grandson that they had a falling out and he hadn't seen her for a couple of days. Now I did call the police and filed a missing person report," Mr. Oh said. "Soon as the police started looking they found that neighbors in DeBain's apartment complex said they heard an argument, heard her shout she was leaving and heard the apartment door being slammed closed. The police found that she had cleaned out her savings account of close to twelve thousand dollars. Police were unable to find a trace of her or the money. Both were gone, disappeared."

Mrs. Oh said, "We told the police that DeBain had hurt her or did something worse. They checked with the airlines and boats leaving the islands, no one remembered seeing her leave. They checked the clinics, hospitals and the morgue, nothing. They talked to DeBain and according to the police report, he told the police the same thing he told our grandson. The police eventually left the case open but believed she had run away after the fight with DeBain. Too embarrassed to come to us. Afraid we would tell her we told her so. Hold it against her."

Mr. Oh said, "We knew she did not run away. She knew we loved her and would not blame her, would take her back."

Willa said, "After a while, we knew. He killed her!"

The conversation on the patio was interrupted by a slight young man with hair down to his shoulders who came from the house and called out 'grandpa'. Mr. Oh introduced him as his grandson, Thomas Oh the Third. He explained that the police were here concerning his missing sister, Connie. The grandson said, "It's about time! You've found something! Found her!?"

Detective Amato said, "No. Just getting more information surrounding the incident."

The grandsons said, "Why couldn't you arrest the bastard! Make him talk! Tell us what he did with Connie!"

Detective Malaki answered him, "Couldn't without proof. Never found a body that possibly could be tied to him."

Detective Amato added, "And now it is too late. DeBain has been killed."

The grandson asked. "Why are you talking to us?"

"We are investigating his murder," replied detective Amato.

Mr. Oh said, "We read in the paper that he had been killed. Has nothing to do with us."

Willa said, "You mean you are here hoping that we can tell you something that will find his murderer!? I spit on him and you!"

"Now mother," her husband said.

"Don't sush me!" Willa spat out. "I hate him and what he done to Connie! I'm glad he is dead!" She got up from the table and said, "I'll be inside. Why don't you two just leave!?"

Mr. Oh said, "I think it best if you go. You've upset mother." The two detectives watched as Mr. Oh went inside. They continued to talk with Thomas Oh the Third for twenty minutes to see if they could get any additional information from him concerning DeBain. They finally concluded that he didn't know anything that would be a help and they left.

CHAPTER 16

SHAFTS OF SUNLIGHT NOW BEGAN TO COME THROUGH THE *upper windows making the interior of the warehouse a little brighter. Small pools of blood had formed in the dust on the floor where bleeding hands have dripped and mixed with the blood from his feet, mouth, urine and the water poured on him. DeBain was breathing hard and his head was bent down. The Unknown Man took a sip of bottled water and offered a drink to DeBain. He did not respond to the offer. He allowed DeBain to catch his breath before the Unknown Man spoke, "I'm almost through asking you about your women and then you will be free." DeBain did not respond to what he heard. He just sat with his head bent down so that his chin touched his chest. The Unknown Man lifted DeBain's head up by putting the hammer's head under the bound man's chin and lift. DeBain opened his eyes and looked at the man torturing, beating him. The torturer let go of the hammer and it fell, but didn't hit the floor The Unknown Man had the leather loop around his wrist. DeBain's head fell back down and his eyes closed when the hammer was removed. The Unknown Man asked, "Don't pass out. Are you listening?" DeBain again did not respond. Unseen by the bound man, his antagonist slipped his wrist from the loop and poured some water on his head. With his free hand, the Unknown Man then took out of his pocket, his pocket knife, set the water bottle down and opened the knife. Taking a half step closer to DeBain he said, "Maybe this will help," and he grabbed the beaten man's ear, pulled it away from his head and cut it off. DeBain tried to cry but he was so worn out he could hardly get any words out. The most that he could do was whimper. His head fell again and he closed his eyes. His whimpering continued as tears formed in the corners of his closed eyes, ran down his cheeks, and dripped off his chin. His chest heaved as blood ran from the cut off ear, ran down his neck and onto his chest where it mixed with the water spilled on him and his tears. The Unknown Man waited a moment and said, "That get your attention?" and he spilled more water on DeBain's head. "You like water, hides your handy work. Tell me how it happened on the beach. What you intended to do?"*

Without lifting his head DeBain said, "Who, who, wha, what?"

"You're mumbling again. Speak up clearly. Don't make me clear your throat," the Unknown Man said. "Concentrate and tell me, what happened on the beach?"

DeBain tried to lift his head and barely got the words out. He paused after each short sentence and caught his breath. He lifted his head enough, opened his eyes and looked at the man in front of him and said, "I'll, I'll tell any' ting want know. Don't 'urt me 'gain. Pleath!"

"Now that's much better," the Unknown Man said.

DeBain's head fell again and his chin touched his chest, "I tole 'er, I was glad we came out here, such a pretty eve'ing. Tole 'er, I love 'er," the beaten man managed to get out as he talked down to his chest. Then he quit talking and was silent.

"Keep going," his torturer said.

"Want run way, marry on money she got. Yeath I tole 'er," DeBain said as he continued to talk to his chest.

"Told her what?" the Unknown Man asked.

DeBain uttered, "Yeath, I love 'er. Any 'ting she want." He paused for a moment while he caught his breath, "Don't 'urt me. Pleath!" he said between breaths as he lifted his head to the Unknown Man. "Pleath! Pleath!"

"Is that what she said? Please don't hurt me," DeBain's torturer asked.

"No, not firs", DeBain answered as his head fell. "I ask 'er, what you tell 'bout 'urt shoulder? She tole 'em twist, getting off boat. They believe 'er. I

tell 'er back fifties a song 'Connie O', some'ting like that. Will find it, be our wedding song. Then I ask, where money? She hold out purse. I pull arm with purse to me. She say I 'urtin' 'er. Tole me it ours, it mine." He was silent. The Unknown Man walked to DeBain's side. He had his pocket knife out and held it low so that the bound DeBain could see it. There was no response. The Unknown Man took hold of DeBain's other ear. He may be hurting, didn't or couldn't respond, but it was clear what was about to happen. DeBain was able to utter, "Don't hurt me. Pleath don't hurt me 'gain." He stopped talking and took a deep breath.

The stranger didn't know if the bound man had passed out so he shook him on the shoulder with the hammer, he asked, "You awake? Don't pass out on me," and he poured a little water on DeBain's head. He said, "Tell me what happened on the beach and her money."

DeBain hadn't passed out, he was just taking a breather and picked up right where he left off, "I never 'urt my Connie Oh I tell 'er. Grab arm, pull to me an' I slap 'er, slap 'er hard!" he said with as much intensity as he was able to muster. "She fell, fell in'a water. I grab purse. Open it. Money there. Fistful of it. She sit up in water, blood run down face. She cough. She look at me. Dumb cow look!" He paused and what would pass as an angry voice said, "She turn on me, ask why I do? Family right, should 'a lis'n them. Tell me I no, no good! I tell 'er, quit crying." He talks to his tormentor, "Pleath mister, please, don't hurt me," and he stopped.

"Go on, please what?" the Unknown Man wanted to know, again shaking DeBain.

DeBain cleared his throat and said, "She tell me, gonna' go ta police, have me 'rested. I went to 'er. Please no. Why do somet'ing like that? You know I love you. Love you more than life, self, I tole 'er." DeBain's tone changed to one of angry disgust, "That when I 'it her! Closed fist! 'It her hard! She fall in'a water. I pull 'er out. Tell 'er, don't look at me those innocent eyes. She know who, what I am. Stop crying I tell 'er again! Push 'er head under surf! What can she do, one arm? Get dark. Tie chain around 'er. Take out, 'bout ten mile and dump over board. She never find."

The unknown Man said to DeBain, "She deserved to be hurt. You taught her a lesson, didn't you?"

Because his eyes were closed, DeBain didn't notice as his antagonist move to his side and he said, "Yes," as the hammer came around and smashed the right unhurt knee. The scream started but was not finished because of the pain, he was unconscious.

CHAPTER 17

THE TWO DETECTIVES CHECKED IN WITH LIEUTENANT Karawa in his office. Moliki Malaki was the first to speak, "Nothing from the Oh family. They hated DeBain, believe that he killed their granddaughter and are glad that he is dead. The grandfather is too old to have done it."

Detective Amato added, "Have a grandson that could have done it, but I doubt it. Not a big man, what you would refer to as a ninety-pound weakling. He didn't look capable physically or mentally. Took someone with a strong stomach to do to DeBain what we saw, or a psycho."

Lieutenant Karawa said, "Give me something to give to the chief. I don't want to tell him the investigation is stalled. If no one connected to DeBain did it, look at Cole again, make sure he didn't take the money. Maybe pay somebody to kill DeBain and scamming his half-brother out of the money. Check who he works with, who he knows, anyone he could have told about the money. Someone had to know!"

Amato asked, "How far can we check into where the money came from. Someone on that end could have done it."

The lieutenant said, "Go where the evidence takes you. Just don't ask questions that could embarrass the department or the governor. Tread lightly. If need be, I'll back you."

"Okay," Amato said, "the Honolulu State, our first stop."

That afternoon they went to the bank's receptionist and identified themselves. She told the two detectives to have a seat. She talked to someone briefly on the telephone and told them vice president, Jimmy Wilson, would be right with them. In a moment, a middle-aged man in his forties came bounding through the lobby. The detectives introduced themselves and asked if they could go somewhere and talk. The vice president did not ask what about, better he didn't know than to have unfounded rumors spread through the bank. Jimmy Wilson said, "Yes, come with me to my office," and he led them through the lobby to the elevator and went up to the second floor and his office. The vice president sat at his desk and the two policemen sat in comfortable chairs across from him. After everyone was settled he asked, "What can I do for you?"

Detective Malaki said, "Need to talk to you about a deposit that was made to your bank."

"I can assure you that everything we do is legal, if this is about drug money we know nothing about it," Jimmy Wilson said in defense of his bank and its practices.

"No, no, nothing like that. A large deposit was made a while back; we want to know who made it."

The vice president turned his computer so that he could see it and touched a key, "Okay, give me the particulars."

Detective Amato said, "Most likely in the past month or so. Would be under the name Cole Bennett, could also be with Philippe DeBain."

After a moment, Jimmy Wilson said, "Sorry, nothing under either. Could it be under a company name?"

Detective Amato pulled out his note pad and looked at it, he said, "Try the West Southeast Trading Company."

The bank's vice president typed in the name of the company and almost immediately said, "Ah, here it is. Yes, deposited on the eighteenth of last month. Quite a large amount. I see here that it has been closed out by one of the two allowed to withdraw it, a Mister Phillipe DeBain."

Detective Amato said, "We know that. What we want to know is where it came from, who sent it. I'm sure it wasn't given to your bank in cash."

Detective Malaki added, "Will also want to talk again to the teller who closed out the account and gave him the money."

"Wasn't just a teller, she had to hand off the request to the manager of that day and he would have verified the identification of the requester, then the transaction would have been concluded and the two of them gave out the money," the vice president said.

Malaki followed up with, "Will need to talk to both of them."

"I'll have both come to my office," he said as he picked up his telephone and talked into it. When he had finished talking on the phone, he looked back at the detectives and said, "In the meantime, says here it was wired from the First National Bank of Hawaii on the main island and drawn on the bank, wouldn't be a name," said Mr. Wilson. "It was good, so never questioned it. If there is a problem, have to talk to them."

Detective Malaki wrote down the information the bank vice president gave them about the wire transfer. There was a knock on the door and Jimmy Wilson invited the teller and her manager in. Both remembered the teller and manager from before. Now they questioned them not as bank employees, but as possible suspects in front of the bank's vice president. Both were satisfied that neither had anything to do with the money's disappearance and the death of DeBain. The detectives got up, thanked all three for their assistance and left.

Shortly the two detectives began looking into the finances of the teller and her manager. They came up blank. If they were involved with taking the money their saving accounts, loans, spending habits and mortgages never showed any unusual activity of late. If either or both were involved they could just wait a half year or more before spending any of the money. If their investigation stalled, the detectives decided that they would come back to them after a time. The case would remain open.

They returned to the station and detective Malaki called the First National Bank of Hawaii and asked to talk to a supervisor. When he said, he wanted information about a money transfer, the bank supervisor told him they would never give out information concerning a customer's transactions over the telephone, policeman or not. They reported in to the lieutenant and were told by their superior to take a plane ride to the big island.

The two detectives were in the office of bank executive Lee Haun on the big island, Hawaii. When they explained that they wished to know where the money came from that the bank wired last month on the eighteenth to the Honolulu State Bank of Oahu, they were told that the bank would not honor the request. It was not bank policy to give out such information unless it was believed the money was gotten illegally and the request was accompanied with a judge's order to do so. Explaining that they were investigating a murder that could be tied to the money got them nowhere. A threat of a possibility of arresting someone from the bank on a hindering an investigation or possibly abetting the murder received the same answer.

They returned to Oahu and asked a judge to give them the permission they wanted to take to the bank. They were told no. They did not have a compelling reason for knowing where the money originated. All of this they reported to the lieutenant. He said he would pass it on to the chief.

Later that day when Amato checked his messages, there was one from the lieutenant that he wanted to see the two of them. They talked to Lieutenant Karawa and explained what they had found, they could find nothing from anyone that knew DeBain or Bennett. That neither had access to that kind of money. Seems they told no one. Their obvious next step was to look at where the money came from, that maybe someone on that end would know about it. When they investigated, they hit a stone wall of the bank's confidentiality. Apparently, the chief passed it on to the governor, and their guess as well as the lieutenant's, were right, that all three of them believed the money came from the governor. The lieutenant got a call from the First National Bank of Hawaii that they would be happy to co-operate in any way they could in the police investigation.

This time Detective Malaki called the bank and talked to the same executive, Lee Haun. Mr. Haun told him, "Sorry about last time, but rules are rules." Detective Malaki said he understood and repeated their original request, where did the money come from. The bank executive said, "According to our records it was transferred from the account of one of our customers to your state bank."

Detective Malaki asked, "We know that, what we want to know is who that customer might be?"

Lee Haun said, "I need you to promise that you will tell no one about the money. Customer wants to keep it quiet." The two detectives said that they would have to report it to their lieutenant but would not put it in any report as long as it was not tied directly to the murdered victim.

In the lieutenant's office, the two detectives were reporting on what they found. Lee Haun informed them the money came from the governor and he wanted it kept quiet. Mr. Haun told them that the governor did in fact give his half-brother the money as a loan. Made him sign a note to that effect. Except for Cole Bennett, no one knew about the money, not even the governor's wife. He wanted it found. Detective Amato said, "So we are back where we started, who killed DeBain and what happened to the money?"

The lieutenant said, "Go back to Cole. Did he mention it to anyone? Did DeBain tell someone? Follow up again on any other women beaten and the cases not solved. Are there any cases of men beaten, maybe killed?"

Malaki said, "We will re-check on women beaten and possible perpetrators. Maybe one of them will come back or point to DeBain. As far as men go, don't think we will find anybody beaten and killed the way DeBain was."

Lieutenant Karawa said, "Keep looking for the money. It just didn't disappear. Find it and we will find his murderer. Someone had to know!"

CHAPTER 18

IT WAS WEDNESDAY MORNING AT THE AMATO HOUSE. MOLIKI Malaki was again waiting for his partner as he threw a toy for the dog to fetch. He ran to get it but would not return it. Detective Malaki said, "Poor fetch dog."

Detective Amato's wife replied, "You know that but you insist on throwing something for him to fetch. Why?"

Moliki's response was simply, "I keep hoping the dog will change its mind"

"You are just like Brian, keeps trying to get the dog to fetch, but it will not," Olana said. "Have to say he is stubborn, just like you. I tell you about one of the single checkers at our store. She's good looking and has a sense of humor and not seeing anyone." There is a pause in their conversation. She was hoping that Moliki was considering her suggestion when she added, "Nice figure too."

Moliki seem to pay no attention to her. The dog trotted over to him. He began scratching the dog's ears but it refused to let go of the toy and it walked away. Finally, he said, "What's that you said?" His hint to Olana that he wasn't listening and she needn't bother trying to fix him up with someone she knew.

Both were silent for a moment when she said, "Brian said he'd be right out but you know how he dawdles. I'll pour you only a half cup."

"No cream," Moliki said.

Olana pushed the container of half-and half across the table to the detective and told him, "Either ignore it or pour as little as you want. You trying to lose a little weight 'cause you got your eye on someone?"

Moliki poured a little cream in his coffee and swirled it around and didn't answer her. "Piece of cinnamon roll," she asked as she slid the plate it was on to the detective. "Watching your figure?" she asked again referring to his weight.

"No. I don't think so," Moliki said. After a moment, he picked up the knife and cut a small piece off. Olana just smiled. "Watching your figure?" she asked again referring to his weight.

As he picked up the piece of roll that he had cut off, Olana said to him, "Brian doesn't talk much about the DeBain case except for your lack of progress. Maybe you should take the dog to help you look."

After he swallowed the piece of roll, Moliki said, "Right now wouldn't hurt. All our prime suspects were people who didn't like him, maybe some had reason to kill him. They all have alibis." At that moment, the dog trotted back to where Detective Malaki was sitting, without the toy. He spoke to the dog, "So, you want your ears scratched again?"

Olana said, "Brian is concerned but not to the degree as other cases. It's an order from above that he solve it, but just between you and me, I think that he wouldn't be upset if it isn't solved. DeBain was not a very nice person from what I've read about him."

"You might be right, but it's a challenge to Brian and he wants closure on it," Moliki said as he took a sip of his coffee.

Olana was silent for a moment and then said, "Have you thought about looking at the people he did not like instead of the other way around?"

"Why do you say that?" Moliki asked her.

"Well," she said, "Ollie knows that the parrot that lives in the neighbor's tree has it in for him, but there's nothing he can do about it. Know what he does?"

Detective Malaki had a puzzled look on his face. What possibly could the dog and a parrot have to do with their case concerning DeBain. He asked, "No, what?"

"He waits on the grass, looks like he is asleep. Birds land on the grass looking for whatever they look for. When they are close enough, he is up and after them. Overtakes the ones that do not get high in the air. Can over take their flight speed. His way of getting even with the parrot. Gets one of the parrot's distant relatives."

Moliki could see no connection to what she just said to their case.

She looked at the dog and continued, "Looking at what you two are doing from the outside, you seem to be focused in one direction, people that didn't like him, hated him or held a grudge. Ollie is smart enough to not just focus on the parrot. There has to be people that you don't know about that he didn't like. Maybe got into an argument with, cheated them, had a beef with him and maybe it escalated, got out of hand."

Moliki though about what she said for a second and said, "That's a thought. I'll run it past Brian and see what he thinks." As he thought about what she just said the dog's tail began to hit the kitchen cabinet as if to give her advice emphasis. He still couldn't see any connection or similarity. Their conversation stopped and he began to rub the dog's ears with less enthusiasm. Moliki took a sip of coffee and changed the subject, "Brian says I won't be seeing you anymore at the grocery store where I shop."

"That's right," she replied. "The corporation is moving me up. I'll be managing the wine department for all their stores. They want me at their headquarters and of course, a big raise."

Moliki said, "That sounds great but what about the occasional cup of coffee in the morning?"

"That we can still do but it may mean you will have to show up earlier," Olana said.

Brian Amato came into the kitchen at that moment and said, "Okay, I'm ready. Let's go. Finish your coffee."

"Thanks, Olana," Moliki said as he finished the coffee in his cup. When they were almost to their car Moliki said, "First stop, I want you to swing by the Beach Parrot Roost," and he tossed the car's keys to his partner. Brian Amato insisted on driving the station's car. Several months ago, after Moliki drove up on a side walk to avoid hitting a bicyclist who shot out of an alley. It was a miracle he didn't hit the bicyclist, but no matter.

"Why," asked Brian Amato.

"Got a few follow up questions for Cole," Moliki said. "Checking on other unsolved cases can wait, they are not going anywhere."

Brian parked in the parking lot and the two detectives entered the bar. As usual, there were several people sitting at the bar. Cole spotted the two detectives at the same time they saw him. Detective Malaki motioned him to come over, saw him say something to the owner and he joined the two detectives and the three of them headed to the rear of the bar and sat at a booth. Detective Malaki was the first to speak, "Any chance that either of you may have casually mentioned what the two of you were planning? Maybe to your boss over there?" He saw Cole shake his head no.

Brian Amato said, "We've checked all of our leads and nothing. You have to help us. Someone DeBain may have mentioned what you were doing, owed money to. Something he may have said."

Cole said, "There were people that knew what we were planning but most thought it was just our dreaming, pie in the sky talking. As far as I know, no one, and I mean no one, knew that we already had the money!"

"Maybe didn't know from you, but what about Phillipe? Could he have mentioned it to someone he knew, a girl he wanted to impress?" Detective Amato wanted to know.

"Girl that he may have been seeing? Easy to slip out in bed."
Detective Malaki said. Cole thought about what he was asked for a
moment as if searching through his mind and just shook his head no.

"You sure he didn't do drugs or gamble?" Amato asked.

Cole replied, "Sure as I can be, he did neither."

Detective Amato said, "The money is gone. What could have happened to it?"

"Anything could be a lead no matter how far-fetched," Detective
Malaki said. "A lot of people we've talked to didn't like him. How about
people he didn't like, avoided?"

"Never mentioned anyone to me that he didn't like or stayed away
from," said Cole. "Only thing I know is, he wanted to avoid that big
parking garage down town."

"He say why?" asked the detective.

"Thought that their clock knocked a few minutes off each hour.
Knew he was in the garage for only an hour but always would be
charged for a full second hour."

"He ever talk to them about it? Rubbed the wrong way when he got
an answer?" Amato asked.

"No, told him to check his watch against the time he checked in
and the time he was leaving," Cole said. "He did and never mentioned
it again. I assumed he was at fault."

"Anything else you can think of? Any people?" detective Malaki
continued.

Cole thought about it for a moment and said, "Don't know what this
may mean, probably nothing. Don't know if I should even mention it."

Detective Malaki said, "What!? Tell us and let us be the judge."

Cole said, "Okay. It was way after lunch time one day and I suggested we have a late lunch at the Tokyo Steakhouse and Sushi Bar. Told
him it didn't open till mid-afternoon. Phillipe said no."

Detective Amato looked at his note pad and said, "The steakhouse
is not on the list of restaurants that you gave us."

"That's because we never went there for lunch. That's why I never told you about it," Cole answered him.

"He say why?" asked Malaki.

All that Cole could say was, "He didn't like the waitresses there."

Brian Amato corrected him and said, "Wait persons. He say why he didn't like the wait people there?"

"No," said Cole, "I didn't ask for a reason, we went elsewhere."

The two detectives were sure they could leave the parking garage off as a place to check. Instead they drove to the Tokyo Steakhouse and Sushi Bar. It didn't open until three in the afternoon so they returned to the station and began checking on unsolved crimes that involved men who were beaten.

There were only two cases that were open, never solved. When they checked on them, they found that the first was a guy who was beaten by three surfers. Talking to him and checking on the police report, the attackers accused the victim of cutting one of them off while surfing. Never did find who any of the three were. The second guy was not so sure he wanted to talk to them about what had happened. He was convinced by the two detectives that they were investigating a murder, not his attack. When he finally did decide to talk, he wanted assurance that what he said would be kept quiet, and he let them know he would not be able to identify his assailant. The detectives found out that the beating was by a woman's boyfriend. Following more questioning they found it was not a boyfriend, but her pimp. The guy would refuse to press charges and for the sake of his marriage, would continue to stick to his story that a guy beat him over a bar argument. The beating would not have even been investigated by the police if a patrolman had not found him outside the bar. The open cases involving beaten women was large and having already started to look at it for the second time the detectives decided to wait and follow up on open cases another day.

After three o'clock the two detectives drove back to the steak house. They were greeted by the hostess and asked their food preference. They showed their credentials and told her they were there on official police business. Detective Amato showed her a photograph of DeBain and asked, "You ever see this guy? Date one of your wait persons?"

The receptionist took the photograph and studied it for a moment and said, "Nope. Never seen this guy with any of our waitresses, but I'm new here. Could have happened before I started," and returned the photograph to the detective.

Detective Malaki said, "Mind if we ask some of your," and he stressed the word, "waitresses?"

"Of course," the receptionist said. Only two work this early, I'll call them. "Nao, Rina, here for a sec."

When the two young women approached the detectives, Amato held out the photograph to them and asked, "Either of you ever seen this guy around here?"

Nao said, "Sure, I think Darby Stewart was seeing him."

Rina held out her hand for the picture, looked at it and said, "Yes. I see him pick her up once or twice."

Detective Amato asked, "Is she working today? We need to talk to her."

"No," Rina said quickly.

At Rina's reply the hostess said, "Hasn't been around for at least two weeks or so."

Detective Amato asked, "Do you know where she lives?"

Nao said, "No, if she's not in the hospital, Taylor might."

Detective Malaki asked, "Who is Taylor?"

"He is one of our cooks," the hostess answered.

Rina added to what Nao said, "They used to hang out together, but haven't seen him around for a while either."

"Why did you say in the hospital Nao" Malaki asked.

She answered, "Darby used to come to work with bruises on her body. I saw them when we were changing into our uniforms. I thought that maybe she had a second job where she was getting hurt."

"Or maybe she was into kick boxing since most of them were not on her face or neck. I saw them too," said Rina.

Nao said, "I asked her about them. She said she fell or walked into something. I didn't want to seem nosey, so I didn't question her about them. Thought it was none of my business. Maybe she was clumsy or careless."

Detective Amato asked, "Could this guy Taylor been beating her?"

"Don't think so," Nao answered. "They hung out a little but I never got the impression that they were close and she never talked about him or them as a pair."

Detective Malaki asked, "What about this guy Taylor? He working today?"

The hostess said, "Like Rina said, haven't seen him for a while either, not since he bought that shiny new red car."

Detective Amato said, "Need his full name and address."

The hostess said, "Last name is Meis, you want to know where he lives, talk to our manager, he should know."

The two detectives drove to the address the steakhouse manager gave them, to where Taylor Meis lived. It was four, two story buildings in a semi-circle around a courtyard. It most likely was quite nice when it was built, but now had been allowed to go downhill. It wouldn't take much to get it back to its original shape though. In the parking lot behind the apartments they looked for a parking space and Amato pulled into one. They got out and walked toward a passage way between two buildings that led from the parking lot to the courtyard and the entrances to the apartments. There in the parking lot they saw a new red Camaro straddling a parking space line so that the spaces on either side were too small for a car to park. Moliki said, "Not going to take too long before someone here figures out what he is doing, keep his car from getting dinged by other car doors. When that happens, some pissed off tenant is going to run a key from the front to the rear of his car."

His partner uttered an, "Uh-huh," in agreement. Once inside the courtyard he said, "Let's look for building D and number 23. Here is A, D probably opposite this one."

They crossed the courtyard, found building D, went inside and checked mail box names and saw T. Meis. They climbed the stairs to the second floor. There were only six apartments in this building so it was easy to find the one they were looking for. They took out their police badges and hung them from their jacket pockets. Not knowing what to expect, the two stood at the sides of the door. Malaki took out his gun and held it at his side, reached to the door with his free hand and knocked.

From inside the apartment they heard a man's voice ask, "Yeah, who is it?"

Detective Amato yelled, "Taylor Meis, police open up!" There was silence for a moment when they heard a noise from inside. Amato recognized it as a window being forced open. "He's going for the window, kick it in!" The two hit the door with their shoulders, felt it being ripped open from the lock and rushed into the room when the door gave way. Malaki aimed his gun at the man half way through the window when Brian Amato grabbed him by the leg and the two detectives began to pull Taylor Meis back into the room. "Where do you think you are going!? Get back in here!" Back inside the room Amato pushed him against a wall, "Hands against the wall where I can see them! Legs apart! Do it!" He began to pat him down.

Taylor said, "What's this all about? I haven't done ..."

And that is as much as he had been able to get out before Detective Amato interrupted him, "What were you running for! What's this!?" and he pulled from the front of Taylor waist a nine mm gun. "You gotta' license for this?" Taylor did not answer him. "I take it the silence means no!" He handed Malaki the gun, pulled one arm down at a time and handcuffed Taylor Meis. When he was turned around they saw a man in his mid-twenties, most likely worked out because of his muscular build, tanned with light brown shoulder length hair and Tay tattoo on one bicep. "We will check you out at the station. In the meantime, you are under arrest for fleeing to avoid arrest and possession of an unlicensed firearm. We will have our tech guys go over the place and see if that is an illegal drug residue in the ash tray. If so, maybe we will add to the charge." They read him his rights and ushered him through the door, closing it as best they could after they left.

They led him down to their car. They passed by the new red Camaro and Amato couldn't help commenting on what they had heard from one of the waitresses, that it was the new car that Taylor had bought and he thought that it was too much car for the island. Taylor didn't respond to the detectives but stayed silent as they placed him in the back seat and headed to police headquarters. Neither spoke to Taylor Meis during the trip. At the station, they put him in the interview room and hand cuffed him to the table. Detective Amato got a uniformed officer to keep an eye on him and the two detectives left. They let him stew for a while as they looked up his police record. They asked another officer to get a judge to sign off on a search warrant for Taylor Meis' apartment. The search was for any illegal drugs and any evidence that would tie Meis to DeBain. They waited for a half an hour and then they returned, let the policeman go and they sat down. Brian Amato opened the file he had and studied it before dropping it on the table so that it hit with a noise. The suspect jumped. He looked at Taylor and said, "I see you've done some petty stuff, shop lifting and an assault."

"Why the gun? Thinking of moving up or have you already made the big move?" Detective Malaki asked.

Taylor Meis answered with, "Why am I here? I haven't done any-thing. Do I need a lawyer?"

Detective Malaki said, "If you want one that is your right, but as you said, you haven't done anything, why would you need one?" The idea was to give him a false sense of security, get him talking and maybe he would say something he shouldn't.

Taylor Meis was silent for a moment, thought about what the detective told him about needing a lawyer and decided to cooperate with the police. Tell them what they wanted to know since he believed that they could not know that he had done anything wrong. Maybe a fine and a warning for the gun. No way could they know about DeBain even though they had mentioned his name.

Amato asked, "Why the gun?"

Taylor Meis said, "I got it for protection."

"Protection from what or from who," asked Detective Malaki.

Taylor said, "Just for protection. I get off work late at night. Made me feel safe."

The two detectives were quiet for a while when Detective Amato said, "Tell us about you and Darby, Phillipe DeBain and the new fifty thousand plus car you just bought."

"I got nothing to say. I don't know what you're talking about. Don't know no DeBain" replied Taylor.

"Well Taylor, your apartment is being searched at this minute. Soon as they find something that ties you to DeBain, you make the big time," Brian Amato told him.

Detective Malaki quickly followed what Amato said with, "Murder one!"

"What happened? You and DeBain argue, get into a fight and you killed him? Maybe you fought over Darby," Brian Amato stated.

Detective Malaki said, "Then you take the money! You are going down for this."

The two detectives could see that Taylor Meis was a little nervous; maybe they were on the right track. Just pressure him a little more, but he gathered himself and said, "What money? I don't know what you are talking about!"

"We will check with the dealership, see how you paid for the car.

If not installments, hope you have a good source for where you got the money," detective Amato said to the young man.

There was a slight knock on the door and detective Malaki got up and went to the door and opened it. Whispering could be heard and he left the room, closing the door behind him. Detective Amato and his suspect sat silently and waited. Taylor Meis finally asked, "What is the chance I can get something to drink?"

Amato said, "We will wait until my partner returns, then maybe a soda."

The two again sat quietly; Amato began drumming his fingers on the table top. After about five minutes the door opened and Detective Malaki entered the interview room. He immediately said to his partner, "Read him his rights again and book him, murder one!" He turned away from Amato and looked at Taylor, a small grin on the detective's face. Detective Amato read him his rights. When he finished, this time he talked to their suspect, "CSI found about fifty thousand dollars at your place and guess whose finger prints were on one of the wrappers of a ten-thousand-dollar bundle of money. I'll tell you, yours and DeBain's!" It wasn't true but the police were permitted to lie to suspects, it was up to the suspect to correct the police.

After he heard his partner's statements detective Amato said to Taylor Meis, "Now is the time to tell us what happened, maybe it wasn't your fault. You argued over Darby and he attacked you and you killed him." Amato knew that DeBain wasn't in a fight with anyone, as the ME said, he was most likely taped to a chair and systematically beaten. But, just like when he told Mr. Locasti that DeBain was beaten in the Locasti style, he embellished statements. If he said something that was not true, let Taylor tell him so. Meis had a lot of money. Maybe it didn't come from DeBain. Let Taylor explain the money. It could be he knew who killed DeBain or helped in the murder. He continued, "You get some, maybe half of the money, your partner gets the rest? You don't tell us, then the whole thing is going to be on you!"

Taylor Meis almost shouted, "No! No! I didn't kill anyone! Don't know what you're talking about! It didn't happen like that!" After the short outburst, he calmed down and asked, "Do I need a lawyer?"

Detective Malaki said, "Not if you didn't do anything. Do you want one? You are entitled to have a lawyer present." He could see Taylor Meis think about what he just said and added, "Just so you know, all of this is being video recorded."

Taylor Meis was silent for a moment as he thought about what the detective had said to him. "No, don't think so. I did not murder anyone, so maybe the best thing is to get this cleared up as soon as possible. Hey! What about my drink?"

Detective Amato said he would go and get a can of soda. On the way through the door Taylor Meis shouted to him that he would like a Coke. Detective Malaki and Taylor Meis waited until he returned with the drink, gave it to Taylor and sat down.

"So, tell us how it did happen," Detective Maliki said to him.

Taylor hesitated, pulled the tab on his Coke and took a long drink and began to tell about him, Darby and DeBain, "It was all her idea."

Amato wanted it clarified and asked, "Who are you talking about? Who is her?"

The suspect said, "Darby. It was Darby's idea."

"Darby who?" asked Detective Amato.

Darby Stewart," said Taylor and he continued talking about the three of them. "DeBain would come into the Steak House occasionally. I never saw him, didn't know who Darby was talking about. I was in the kitchen cooking. Darby told me he hit on her every time she was there and that he always had a lot of money, left her a big tip. She told me about his gold tooth with a big flashy diamond set in it. Said he bragged about how much it cost, like it was a big deal. She came to me. Said we should get some of his money."

Detective Amato asked Taylor, "So you two planned on robbing him?"

"No! No!" Taylor said, "It wasn't like that," as he took a sip of his soda.

"If it wasn't like that, tell us what it was like," the detective said.

Taylor Meis continued, "Darby said she had a plan, how we could get some of his money, and we could share it. You can film us she said. Like a dummy, I didn't know what she was talking about. Had to explain it to me. I told her yeah, I can get hold of a movie camera. Told her he was a business partner of the half-brother of the governor and told her he could do her some good. Wanted to take her home but she kept putting him off. He kept after her, saying he could show her how he could help her, just wanted the opportunity to explain," as he took another sip of his drink.

"So, what happened?" detective Malaki asked.

"We get set, I'd hide in her closet and the camera was on a tripod. It covers her bed. Can see through the slats on her closet door. All I got to do is turn it on. I put a piece of tape over the red light that told you it was recording. We do a test run and look at it. It was perfect. All she had to do was make sure he didn't turn off the lights in the room and I'd film them. She finally said okay to DeBain's invite to give her a ride home. Told me she'd tell me when she would be ready, just wait. Gave me a key to her place. She confessed to me he'd already taken her home once or twice for a couple of weeks. I was a little surprised, but it was okay with me. Really none of my business what she did with him or any other guy. So, I did. I don't have to tell you his plan for doing her some good. In no time, he was banging her, his idea of helping her. She told me he liked to get rough. I'm not sure if it wasn't her idea for him to get rough with her. After I saw them the first time the thought crossed my mind, maybe why she let him take her home a couple of weeks before she asked me to film them. I'm nervous as hell the first time, hiding in her closet, but all I had to do was be quiet, turn the camera on and film them."

Amato interrupted Taylor's story and asked, "What about the lights?"

Taylor Meis took a short break in his explanation and took a drink from his can of soda. Then he said, "Turned out, both wanted to keep the lights on. He wanted to be able to see her and according to her she wanted to see the look in his eyes when he was with her. She was right, he did like to get rough. He slapped her around a bit, nothing above the neck. Saw him bite her on the tit, made it bleed. He slapped and punched her in the stomach and on her sides but not too hard. Made her turn over and started to slap her on the ass. He also bit her there too. Like a dummy when we did our test run, I didn't turn on the sound, didn't know how to do it and was afraid if I started to fool around looking for it in the darkened closet I might make noise. After the first time, we looked at what was filmed and it was perfect, clear and easy to see DeBain. I told Darby about the sound and she said to leave it off."

Detective Amato asked, "Why do you think she didn't want sound?"

"A week later she comes back into the kitchen where I'm cooking and tells me to get set up for the next night after work and asks if I still had the key to her place," said Taylor. "She will stall him by asking him to buy her a drink. Had to keep him out until I got off work and was able to get to her place. That night it became clear why she didn't want the sound. After he slapped her around a little she turns away from the camera and began to encourage him. Why I thought it may have been her idea. Couldn't see her mouth but I heard her, hit me again, harder and again, harder she yells to him. DeBain starts to hit her harder. It looked to me that he was getting tired when she yelled to him, do it now, fuck me, fuck me hard. Make it hurt. Oh, yes, she yells, fuck me now. Hit me she tells him, harder. And he does. She moaned so loud I thought she'd wake up everyone in her building. Then he puts his hands around her neck. Didn't know if he was trying to keep her quiet or was he going to strangle her. Thought I might have to break out of the closet when he stops."

Malaki asked, "How did you plan to get it, the money?"

Taylor said, "That was supposed to be easy, black mail him with the film. We thought with him doing her and beating her, it would be enough. He really got into it, the beating. I didn't film all their meetings. And now I have the sound on. Looking at some of it we can hear the slaps and her crying sometimes. After a while he began to punch her different places on her body, she would moan and sometimes cry. Took off his belt and would hit her on the back and her ass. Not hard enough to leave a scar. Darby would show me the bruises. Had me film them up close. He would squeeze her tits so hard they had bruises on them."

"But something went wrong," Amato said. "Darby gets hurt?"

"No," replied Taylor. "None of the beating was that serious. She told me it hurt when he hit her, but it wasn't too bad, but each time he does hit a little bit harder she said. I thought that we should stop then. But Darby didn't want to. She was sure that she could take it a little bit longer as long we were going to get money from him in the end. I think that she was beginning to like the beatings. We talked about him strangling her. I thought he was going to kill her. She said she made it clear to him, no more strangling."

Detective Malaki said, "But you got upset, him doing your girl, hurting her."

"I told you! She wasn't my girl!" Taylor Meis said with finality in his voice. "It gets better."

"How so?" Amato wanted to know.

Taylor takes a drink of his soda, pushed back in his seat and grinned at the two detectives and said, "I think this has been going on for about a month and a half now and she gets knocked up! At least that's what she told me. Tells me to record them when she tells him. I agree. So, next time before they even start she tells him she is pregnant. At first, he is surprised. How do I know it is mine, he asked her? She tells him she hasn't been with another guy for several months. DNA will prove it. He quickly recovers and he told her to get an abortion. She tells him in no uncertain terms, no! I think he was surprised at her answer and says to her, No! She just looked at him and said nothing. Now he tells her he'll hit her so hard in the stomach she won't need an abortion. I think she believed him so she agreed but told him he will have to pay for it. He gave her a couple of hundred dollars and left. There was no action that night for me to film, only the confrontation."

"Was she?" asked detective Malaki.

"I don't know," replied Taylor and he continued. "She was not satisfied with a few hundred dollars. She wanted more, wanted to stick to the original plan. She wanted to know if I could get a gun. I thought she meant for us to rob him, when she said just to be on the safe side. I tell her no problem and that's where the gun came from. She arranges to meet him in a few nights and tells him he should pay or she is going to have him arrested for beating her. She asks for a quarter million dollars. I had no idea he had this much or that we could get it. Don't know how she knew. At first, he challenges her, tells her he will deny he ever touched her. Wanted to know what proof she had. I'm surprised when she calls to me and I came out of the closet. We showed him some of the film. That is when she added to what she threatened, with the fact that she didn't have an abortion and that the baby's DNA couldn't be denied. It becomes public who knows how this will affect his deal with the governor's half-brother."

"He decided to pay? How much?" asked Brian Amato.

Taylor said, "Not at first. He balked. That's when we showed him more of the film and the bruises on Darby. We had made the bruises look worse with some make-up she had. Darby threatened him to either pay up or go to jail and end any kind of deal he might have with the governor's half-brother. He stared at her for a second and I could see the vein on his forehead swell and he began to turn red. He clinched his hands into fists called her a bitch and threatened to kill her. He took a step toward her, that is when she told him that if he touches her again that I would put him in the hospital. I thought he was going to kill her when he turned toward me. He was quickly sizing me up, I thought that I could take him, but I wasn't sure. He called me a rat-fuck and said he'd take care of me first. That's when I moved my shirt aside and let him see the gun I had tucked in my belt. I put my hand on the butt. He made a complete turn around and was silent. I could swear that I saw him get smaller right there before my eyes."

"So, what happened next between the three of you," Detective Amato wanted to know.

"It was now time for Darby to get even with him for what he had done to her," Taylor said. "She told him that we would meet him in the restaurant's parking lot tomorrow at noon and he better not try anything funny. He is not there, at twelve thirty, she will be walking into the police station, and ordered him to get out of her apartment. DeBain begged for more time, said he couldn't get that kind of money in such a short a time. Darby wouldn't hear it, she again said to him, tomorrow or else. I figured he had either told her or hinted that he could get his hands on that kind of dough."

"What did you two do then?" detective Amato wanted to know.

Taylor said, "Darby insisted that I stay the night, just to be on the safe side and I slept on her sofa."

"What took place the next day?" Malaki asked.

Taylor Meis said, "We got there 'bout an hour early and waited. At about a quarter after, maybe twelve thirty, he pulls into the parking lot and stops. Darby walks to his car and I'm about ten feet behind her. I move to her side making sure my shirt is pulled to the side so that he can see the gun. I heard her ask, where is it. DeBain answered with, he could only get two hundred thousand. She told him to not get out and to keep his hands where I could see them. She told him to hand the money to me and he passed a small travel bag through the window. I stepped closer to the car and grabbed it and stepped back. I zipped it open, I'd never seen so much money before, hundred dollar bills all wrapped in neat packets. She looked over at me then down to the bag that I held open and pointed toward her. She smiled and took a step closer to the car. I had no idea what she was going to do. That is when I heard DeBain say, the film. She put her hand out to me and I placed the camera in it. She reached out to the car and handed the camera to DeBain and at the same time said, something to remember me by, and with a closed fist hit him on the jaw. Now, take off she told him, and he drove out of the lot."

"What did you do with the money?" Amato asked.

Taylor finished his soda and said, "We went to my place and counted it. Sure enough, just like he said, two hundred thou'. Darby wanted more than half since she was the one getting beaten, but in the end, we split it down the middle as planned."

"Where is Darby? Want to talk to her, see if she backs up your story," Detective Malaki said.

Taylor answered him, "Darby didn't want to go home. She had me drop her off at a friend's place. Next day I get a call from her from the airport, she is on her way to California, San Fran'."

"When was this?" Amato wanted to know.

"Two weeks ago, last Saturday," Taylor told him. "Check with the airlines, they will have a record of her leaving. She was afraid of him and didn't trust him. Neither did I, the reason for the gun."

"What happened to the film? You keep it?" Detective Malaki asked.

"No," replied Taylor. "He wanted the film for the money. We traded for it. Gave him the camera with the DS card still inside it. Neither one of us trusted him, why she took off."

"What do you think lieutenant," Malaki asked the lieutenant after the interview.

"Heard most of it through the glass, could be telling the truth. Sure would like some way to back up his story though."

The trip to the airline backed up Taylor's story about Darby leaving. "The airline confirmed part of his story. The girl did leave as he said, but not to San Francisco, to Chicago," Detective Amato said. "The girl at the counter remembered her, said she paid with new hundred dollar bills for a one-way ticket. We also have it on tape."

Lieutenant Karawa said, "If he got the film, bet he didn't destroy it. Search his office and apartment again, also look for any place else he might own, rent or have access to. See if you can locate the camera. Did he have a safety security box? Check with all the banks and anyone else that may rent security boxes."

CHAPTER 20

THE UNKNOWN MAN ASKED, "ARE YOU CONSCIOUS? MAYBE *confused? Catch your breath so we can talk. Maybe this'll help." He poured water on DeBain's head and shook him on the shoulder.*

DeBain tried to lift his head, couldn't, and asked, "Why? Why doing this ... me? Pleath, pleath thop. You don' know me ..." DeBain struggled to get the words out, "I'll pay ..., pay more ..., pay more you getting ..., fifty thousan' ... Le' me, let go." Blood dribbled out of his mouth and ran down his chin.

The Unknown Man uttered, "Hummm. In a little while. I'll have to think about the money. But you've seen me!"

DeBain struggled to speak, "I 'wear, 'wear to God, I won', won' 'member you."

The stranger said to DeBain, "You said you'd sue."

"No, no I won'," said DeBain. Then he asked, "This 'bout Darby? Wasn't my fault. She ask me to. You 'nother frin hers. Darby get even?" The Unknown Man didn't say anything, he just looked at DeBain and waited for him to continue. After a moment, he struggled but was able to get out, "I, I gave money. Didn't hurt that bad, ask 'er. She ask it." He fell silent. "Why, why doing this me? Pleath thop."

"Don't want to hear about Darby. Tell me about the woman on the beach. The receptionist. Is that what she said? She ask, why are you doing this to me? Please stop. But you wanted to get even with all women. Right?"

"Don' know what talkin' 'bout," said DeBain. "Not hurt anyone."

The Unknown Man tapped DeBain on the shoulder with the hammer head and asked, "What did I say about lying? The girl on the beach. You hurt her. You going to also kill her?"

To the best of his ability DeBain said, "No! No!"

"You weren't going to drag her into the water and drown her?" the Unknown Man asked.

"No! No! Never do dat," DeBain replied again talking to his chest. "Pleath."

The Unknown Man spilled a little more water on DeBain's head and said, "You telling me the truth? I'm going to hurt you if you are lying! You don't want me to hurt you, do you?

"No, No. Pleath," the bound man uttered. The Unknown Man swung the hammer in front of DeBain. He saw it and knows what is about to happen. "Yeath, yeath. I gonna' drown 'er!"

"Tell me about her and you. Don't leave anything out," the Unknown Man said.

DeBain struggled, cleared his throat, spit out blood and was able to get out, "Yeath, I gonna' drown 'er. I sorry. Pleath!"

The Unknown Man said to his captive, "Take your time, think about what happened and tell me about her."

DeBain was quiet for a moment and had to be prodded to tell his torturer what he wanted to know concerning the girl on the beach. A poke on the side where he had been hit got him talking, "Had me, had me 'rested! Slut!"

"Who had you arrested?" the Unknown Man asked.

"She did, bitch 'ceptionist! Danni," the bound man said. "Took my money, get even."

"Who took your money? The receptionist?"

"Yeath, Darby, no Danni. Get even with her," DeBain was able to utter. "She away, but not Danni."

"What did you do, how did you go about it?" he asked DeBain.

DeBain hesitated for a moment and uttered, "P'anned it. P'anned it good. Can't take any chances. Need saw at movies. See it elsewhere so can 'scribe it

if asked. Need a disguise, if anyone see me, won't be 'dentified. Will be suspect,
'cused. Need alibi. Pick night she work late," and he stopped talking.

The Unknown Man told him to continue, "How did you plan it good, and
the alibi?"

It is almost with pride when DeBain described what he did. He perked
up and his speech became clearer but his sentences were chopped when he
spoke. He even lifted his head enough so that he could see his antagonist.
"I go to movie, wear flowery shirt, white slacks. Wait near popcorn being
soll. Woman wit daughter buy large tub, ask, ext'a butter. They head, head
for en'rance, I quick to follow. When near security camer', bump into her,
spill popcorn. I quick, yell at her, loud, curse her, make scene. Butter on my
slacks, she pay to clean I yell! She yell back, not her fault, I bump into her.
We yell each other."

DeBain stopped talking. The Unknown Man didn't know if he was catching his breath, taking a break or maybe he passed out. He spilled some water
on DeBain's head and asked, "You relishing the moment, how clever you are?"
He could see a small grin cross the bound man's face when DeBain tilted his
head up to look at the Unknown Man.

The water brought DeBain back to reality of the warehouse and the small
compliment the Unknown Man paid him. He could see that DeBain was relishing his cleverness. DeBain kept his head up and continued. "We creating a
scene. Theater manager come to us and calm down. She a cute thing, maybe
come back, ask out. Think since manager, she ..."

The Unknown Man hits DeBain on the shoulder with the hammer to get
his attention and said to him, "Get back to Danni, the girl on the beach!"

"Huh?" said DeBain as he cleared his head and tried to remember what he
had been talking about. Again, he spat out blood. "Manager, she say can thee
no stain my pants. Offered new popcorn. They go to popcorn coun'er. I go into
movie." DeBain's head slumped and then he continued to talk to his chest. "See
it otter movie. I smart. May be asked 'bout it. Been here before, sit near exit
door. Inset in wall and covered with a black curtain. Wait for dark scene in
movie. Up, through curtain and wait. Loud scene, I open door 'nought to slip

through and I outside in the dark. I change clothes an' go to 'er hotel. Don' care her boyfriend has gun. I make pay. May after smart ass frien too."

"Who are you talking about? Danni?"

"No, no, Darby. She a bitch," he mumbled. He stopped talking.

It took another hammer push to the foot and the Unknown Man again told him to continue, "Tell me about the girl on the beach, Danni, not about Darby."

DeBain tried to lift his head. "Call, ask for fron' desk. Tell hotel 'brella being blown out to ocean. Will send someone to get it. I know it be her. I wait, put on mask. Thee 'er. She look for 'brella. Not see me behin'. Hit 'er! Knock 'er down! Grab aroun' neck, choke! She pass out. Drag to water. Whoever know? Bitch an' boyfriend come beach. I run." His head fell to his chest.

The Unknown Man took a step to DeBain's side. His head down, DeBain heard his torturer ask him if he remembered what he said about Jennifer. When he didn't answer, he was told, "You said she meant everything to you. You lied." DeBain did not see the Unknown Man as he began to swing the hammer in a sideways arc. "I lied too," was the last thing he heard. The hammer hit DeBain on the side of his face. The hammer head caught him high on the cheek. Teeth were knocked out, facial bones broken as DeBain's head whipped back from the blow. More blood from his mouth and his now broken jaw. There was no movement when the Unknown Man swung the hammer again and this time hit him on the back of his head, just behind the ear and killed him. The Unknown Man continued what he began to say, "I'm not going to let you leave."

CHAPTER 21

THE TWO DETECTIVES AND THEIR LIEUTENANT WERE IN the lieutenant's office looking at a computer monitor. On the monitor, they saw Darby, a pretty girl in her early twenties, tanned with very short dark hair with a touch of red to it. Detective Malaki said, "Guess the kid wasn't lying about the girl and DeBain."

Lieutenant Karawa, "Who would have guessed that such a pretty innocent young thing had such an evil streak in her? And DeBain, who would have guessed that he was that into beating women? Looks like they both liked it."

Detective Amato said, "We get to meet them all at one time or another."

Lieutenant Karawa asked, "Where did you find it?"

Detective Malaki said, "The camera was on a bookshelf but no memory DS card in it. Bottom drawer of his desk had a false bottom. Once we took out all the papers that were in it, was easy to spot. Found fifty thousand there also. If the kid was telling us the truth that DeBain paid two hundred thousand, the governor gave Cole two hundred and forty, don't know where the extra ten came from. Maybe from the stock firm. If it did, no idea where the rest of the thirty thousand went. It would be gone. Now that DeBain is dead probably never know."

"Maybe we can give some of it back to the victims we now know he robbed. Cole will want all of it," Lieutenant Karawa said.

Detective Amato said, "Checked with the Chicago police and the airlines. No evidence where she went once she reached Chicago. Issued an arrest warrant for her, but she is gone. Chicago police are not going to spend a lot of time looking for her, and if they do get her, all we can do is arrest her for black mail. Is it worth it?"

"Or she will deny everything that the kid said, say DeBain paid her to go away. How can we prove otherwise? At least we know what happened to the money, it was not why he was murdered," detective Malaki said.

"And if the kid's lawyer tells him to go along with what she says, then what?" Detective Amato added.

"Plus, a lot of the money is already gone. Should be able to get some back from the kid and resell his car, but Darby's share is a different story, even if we can find her," Detective Malaki said.

Lieutenant Karawa said, "I think that what you are saying is true, but I'll pass it along and let others decide whether to pursue her and the money. In the meantime, we still have a murder to solve."

"We know DeBain wasn't killed for the money. So why was he killed?" detective Amato asked.

"Tomorrow start over with the suspects you already have," Lieutenant Karawa said, "the latest would be a good place to start, the Meis kid. Talk to the girl on the beach who accused him of beating her! Find out who did it and why he was murdered."

Detectives Amato and Malaki entered the lieutenant's office and reported Thursday morning's findings. Detective Amato said, "Same as last time, the girl who was attacked on the beach is out of the hospital recovering at home but could tell us nothing. We are a standstill with her. Interviewed people at her hotel and got nowhere. Checked with anyone that may have known her, anyone she may have dated, nothing.

Taylor never heard DeBain mention anyone he might have known. No idea where Darby might have gone. If DeBain told her about the money he had, she could be a help. Maybe other things he told her in bed. Interviewed people at her apartment and got nowhere."

Lieutenant Karawa asked, "What about the doctor?"

Detective Malaki answered, "He refused to talk to us. We want to ask him questions, he gave us his lawyer's phone number and told us to go through him."

"Locasti's personal secretary told us to come back with a warrant we want to talk to his boss and he had nothing to add to what he had already told us," detective Amato added.

"What about Cole Bennett?" the lieutenant asked.

Detective Malaki answered, "Same with him, nothing. Talked to anyone he may have known or may have known about him and DeBain's plans. No one he could remember that hated DeBain other than the two he told us about. According to him, he told no one, not even his boss at the Parrot's Roost or any of the regulars that Cole could have told. If DeBain told anyone, it had to be Darby. Maybe the kid was correct, DeBain told the girl, Darby. A friend got even for her. She had the money to pay someone. A warning to make sure he wouldn't come after her got out of control."

Detective Amato said, "We will talk to Darby's friends, men she had dated, see what we can come up with.

After two days, the two detectives were in the lieutenant's office and had explained that investigating Darby's friends had gotten them nowhere. "We will move on," the lieutenant said. "I got a thanks from the chief to pass on to you. If we find the murderer fine, if not, well, we don't. DeBain was not a nice guy. I guess the chief and the governor are satisfied with the case and what I gave them. I am keeping the file open on the murder but I'm assigning you two to a new case."

That afternoon detective Amato got a call on his cell phone. He answered it and heard Lieutenant Karawa, "Something has come up that

I want you to check out. Go to a vacant warehouse on the commercial B docks, number seventeen. A sergeant and couple of dock officers will be waiting for you. Seems that the owner of the warehouse found something and stopped a couple of beat officers to check it out. They did and called their sergeant who then called me. Said it looks like a pool of dried blood and a tape recorder."

Detective Amato asked into the phone, "What is this in connection with?"

He heard Lieutenant Karawa say, "It's a long shot, but a sergeant on the scene said it may have something to do with the DeBain killing. You and Malaki check it out and then we will know. Get back to me."

Detective Amato drove to the B docks and they began looking for warehouse number seventeen. Detective Malaki pointed to where two police cars were parked. Detective Amato drove to it, saw the number seventeen on the loading dock door, parked and they got. They walked to the open garage door where a policeman was standing. They showed their badges and the policeman escorted them into the warehouse with its overhead lights on. As they walked to where they saw other policemen near a stack of wooden pallets, Amato asked his escort, "You one of the guys who found it?"

Their policeman escort told him, "Yes."

"How'd you find it?" asked Detective Malaki.

"Owner was going to rent half of this space so he and the new renter were checking it out. It had been advertised to rent for the past two weeks. Told us the previous renter left almost a month ago. Said they saw what you are about to see. It looked suspicious and he called us in. The new renter took off before we got here but we do have his name and address. The owner told us this was the second call he had gotten concerning the warehouse. That's him in the shorts with the sergeant."

On the other side of the wood pallets the sergeant called to them, "Over here detectives, this is what you were called about," and he pointed to a chair that looked like it was in a pool of dried blood that had two drag marks around and through it and shoe prints. Scattered about were pieces of torn duct tape. Away from the pool of blood was a stool and on it, a tape recorder.

Detective Amato immediately took in the scene and asked, "Anyone touch anything?"

The sergeant said, "No. Didn't know what had happened but thought someone should investigate. This sure looks like dried blood."

The policeman that was near the sergeant pointed to a small white object close to a marker outside of the blood dried area and said, "This looks like a tooth. That is when we decided to call it in and get a sergeant down here."

Detective Amato asked, "What about the tape recorder?"

The sergeant answered Detective Amato, "We started to listen, but after we heard what was on the beginning, we called it in."

Detective Amato said, "So you did touch the recorder."

The sergeant said, "Been a sergeant lot'a years, know better than that. Pressed the play button with the tip of my pen."

"Well, do it again, let's hear what's on it," said Amato to the sergeant.

The sergeant took out his pen and pushed down on the rewind, when it stopped he pushed the play button. There was a moment of silence and then from the recorder clearly was heard, *"Do you want to tell me anything Mister DeBain?* It was quickly followed by a defiant voice, *"No! I want a lawyer! Somebody is going to be sued!* The original voice was heard to say, *"I believed that you would say that so I have a message from one of your lady friends. Ever think that what you did hurt? Hurt a lot?"* There was a moment of silence when they heard a noise they cannot identify then another. The sergeant pushed down on the stop button.

Detective Malaki said, "If I had to guess I'd say the chair, and maybe DeBain who was on it, were tipped over onto the floor. The second sound was muffled, like through a gag. Let's hear a little more."

Again, the play button was pushed and a moment of silence. Then the original voice could be heard, *"That hurt, maybe this will take your mind off it.*" This time a definite thud could be heard and the group of police were sure they could hear a muffled scream followed by silence.

Detective Amato said to the sergeant, "We've heard enough. Turn it off. Don't anyone touch anything and don't step on the dried blood or foot prints. I'm calling CSI to get here and let them follow up."

The warehouse owner asked, "When can I rent it?"

Detective Amato said, "This is now officially a crime scene. Only time will tell."

The following morning the two detectives were sitting in the lieutenant's office. On Lieutenant Karawa's desk sat the tape recorder. The three had listened to it for the second time. Lieutenant Karawa finally said, "I'll be damned. That tape clears up some of the accusations that have been made about DeBain. Can give closure to a couple of families."

"Clears some of our unsolved cases too. Guess we should inform the police in Malaysia about the two dead strippers he talked about," Detective Amato said. "Doubt it could be used in a court of law though," he added.

Detective Malaki said, "CSI identified it was DeBain's blood and tooth on the floor as well as on the chair arms. They are sure the drag marks in the blood were where his feet were dragged, could get nothing identifiable from the shoe prints. Pretty much tells us why he was killed and where."

"Question is, who did it?" Lieutenant Karawa asked. "Not a finger print or anything at the scene that wasn't DeBain's. Either of you recognize the voice. Maybe someone you talked to?"

Detective Malaki replied, "No. Don't recognize it."

"Could be anyone," said detective Amato. "I want to talk to everyone again, starting with the girl on the beach, his last victim. Whoever beat him kept alluding to the girl on the beach, had to be her."

"Or she could have been the last straw before someone decided to do something about this woman beater," Lieutenant Karawa said. "What about the boat owner Wang's cousin?"

"Never talked to him, don't know what he sounds like. Don't know how good his English is either. It will be good if what we heard about him is true and he has a dual citizenship passport," Detective Amato said. "He would also know about the warehouses on the docks. Someone had to know it was empty and how to get into it and lure DeBain to it."

"Owner said he advertised it and DeBain was the only person he talked to about it. He talked to him about it over the phone. They talked about size and rental cost. He never saw DeBain in person or heard from him after their initial talk," Detective Amato said.

"You know," Detective Malaki began, "Wang's cousin is the one person possibly connected to this we never talked to. Cousin could have done it. But, most of the people we talked to could easily have hired someone to do it, including Wang. Then there is the missing grandfather and his relatives."

"Two problems with the cousin theory," Detective Amato said. "First, anyone who knows Wang said the cousin did go back to China. Chinese aren't going to look for him when all we can say to them is, he is someone we would like to talk to. If they did locate him, doubt they will want to turn him over to us for such a flimsy reason. Second, any money Wang made from smuggling he quickly spent. Had to borrow money against his boat and had a PD represent him in court. Makes us believe that the cousin was the one behind the smuggling and got a larger share of the money made. Checked the visitor log and he didn't have any. Only telephone calls made were between him and his PD lawyer. Chinese family will be difficult to find, and if we do, they will be tight lipped."

"Well do a quick look and then get back to the new case I assigned you," Lieutenant Karawa said.

Detective Amato said, "Have a slight lead I want to check on. The guy at her hotel we talked to, Raymond Lakaa, was over friendly with her. Did some checking on him. No police record but found that he worked on the docks for a couple of years. Hurt his back and had to find a job that didn't require heavy lifting. Would know about warehouses."

It was before noon on Saturday and the hotel guest, Ben Knight, was checking out. The reservationist asked, "How was your stay Mister Knight? I hope that everything was to your liking."

Ben Knight answered her, "It was perfect. If you would call me a cab and a bell boy to get my bags now that I've checked out, I would be appreciative."

"Mister Knight, leaving our island?" said Detective Malaki in a friendly voice.

Turning toward the voice Knight recognized the detectives who had questioned him. "Yes detective," he said. "I'm afraid paradise is over and it's back to the real world. I hope you've made progress on your case with Danni's accused attacker and his murder."

"We have a few leads we are checking on," detective Malaki said. "We'll get our man eventually."

Knight could hear them talk as they walked away. He heard the friendlier of the two ask his partner why he couldn't come to his place for a cook out. Before they were out of hearing range he heard Detective Malaki answer, "If you must know, I have a date with Nikki."

There was no response from the other detective, and then, "Here he comes now, let's talk to him," Detective Amato said to his partner.

Raymond was walking through the lobby toward the two detectives and past Knight when he spotted the guest standing near his bags. He was quick to recognize the man who had been friendly to him and was aware he was checking out. "Aloha, Mister Knight, I mean Ben. Come back," he said in a very warm voice.

"I hope to do that Raymond," Knight replied as he watched the two detectives go toward the hotel employee. They reached him and Detective Malaki began to guide him out of the reception area. He could hear them ask about a place where they could talk and heard Raymond suggest the empty dining room. The three headed in that direction. When they were out of sight Knight asked the reservationist, "Does Raymond work every day?"

She was quick to answer, "As far as I know he only has Sundays off. He has a big family to take care of and puts in a lot of over time, ten hour days."

"Well, I liked him," said Knight.

"Most of the staff do. Heard you mention Danni," she said.

"I did," said Knight. "How is she doing?" he asked with concern in his voice.

The reservationist said, "What an ordeal she went through. But, she has recovered well enough so that she will be back next week. We've heard that when she heard her accused attacker, DeBain, was dead, her spirits picked up and she couldn't wait to return."

Knight said, "That's great news. I've tipped most of the staff; can I leave something for her? A small gift for being so helpful." He pulled from his pocket a small gift wrapped box and an envelope and handed it to the reservationist.

She took the envelope and then the small gift. She said, "I'll just put them in her mailbox."

More than a week had passed and Danni had returned to work. All the staff that knew her welcomed her back. Especially happy to see her was Raymond. "Miss Kayleu it is so good to see you. Welcome back."

Danni replied, "Thank you Raymond and I can't tell you how much I appreciated you coming to see me in the hospital. You really cheered me up."

"And I hear that your attacker is dead," Raymond said to her

"Yes," she replied, "and it may not be Christian, but I thank God he is dead."

Raymond left Danni and walked out to the pool and she checked her mail box. She pulled a handful of letters and hotel notices. The last thing she removed was a small gift wrapped box. To no one in particular she asked as if talking to herself, "What is this?"

A male reservationist said to her, "I believe one of the guests left it for you."

She walked away and flipped through the mail she had received. Most of it was from friends or hotel staff welcoming her back. The hotel notices she quickly scanned and threw in a trash receptacle. Then there was the sealed envelope with no name on it. She tore it open and found a single folded piece of hotel paper. When she unfolded it, all that was written said, 'Because you were so nice to me'. She stuck it with the rest of her mail when she reached her desk. She sat and began to unwrap the small gift. Inside the wrapping paper was a small ring box. She opened it. On a piece of purple velvet was a gold tooth with a diamond set in it.

The End

Printed in the United States
By Bookmasters

Printed in the United States
By Bookmasters